JAZZ FUNERAL

JAZZ FUNERAL

REVENANT FILES™ BOOK THREE

D'ARTAGNAN REY
MICHAEL ANDERLE

DISRUPTIVE IMAGINATION

THE JAZZ FUNERAL TEAM

Thanks to our Beta Team:
Kelly O'Donnell, Larry Omans, John Ashmore

Thanks to our JIT Team:

Wendy L Bonell
Dave Hicks
Dorothy Lloyd
Zacc Pelter
Angel LaVey

If we've missed anyone, please let us know!

Editor
SkyHunter Editing Team

LMBPN Publishing
PMB 196, 2540 South Maryland Pkwy
Las Vegas, NV 89109

Version 1.01, November 2021
eBook ISBN: 978-1-68500-567-2
Print ISBN: 978-1-68500-568-9

CHAPTER ONE

The sky was a purple hue, the color of royalty. He had grown to loathe it. The now-former keeper sat on a throne that was not his and looked at a valuable treasure he had hidden away. He had bought himself some time, but he knew it would not last. His brother would come at some point or send his new pets after him, but he would be prepared.

He looked at his hands. The red glow was much lighter than before and his powers were fading fast. He balled them into fists, fell to his knees, and pounded them onto the floor. Dark figures erupted from the shadows and flew out of the throne room and through the temple. The flames were extinguished as more left and raced into the jungle outside.

Kriminel closed his eyes and tried to reach out to his pet, but the Axman would not respond. He couldn't even feel him. Was that cocky fool already dead? For all his grandstanding and time wasted on complex plans, he was nothing without his benefactor's power. But where did that leave the loa? He no longer had his keeper status and he knew what his fate would be once he was caught.

With a growl, he pushed to his feet and approached the totem that hovered above him. The shield that protected and trapped it cost him most of his remaining power. It seemed he found himself awaiting the end—was that his reality? Had his grand design been undone by the meddling of his brother and some freaks who fancied themselves detectives?

Frustration gnawed at him as he marched to the throne room and collapsed into the chair, his dark creations flanking his sides. Here, he could still believe himself king —what he believed he should have been instead of wasting his potential on the trite duties of a keeper. They could be so much more but settled for an existence as glorified ferrymen for the dead. It seemed he was the only one who still dared to dream.

He looked at the totem, his one saving grace. If he could take it for himself, he would have his powers back. He could get his minion in line again and this could all be saved. That hope was what kept him going. He wasn't only doing this for himself but the fears of others held him back. This pointless cycle needed to end. It would not be Armageddon but would be life born anew.

But for now, he waited. Someone would come, he was sure of it. He would be ready and prepared this time. He knew that he only needed a little more time and nothing could stop him. At least that was what the loa told himself. He needed to believe that and the cold voice that mocked him in his mind had to be silenced.

And yet he could not stop his hands from shaking. Something was coming.

"This is Agent Donovan," the man said crisply as he reported in. "I'm here at the Axman's theater hideout with a team of over a dozen agents and the fire department. We are still clearing the rubble from the fire, but we have not found any clues to where the Axman may be hiding now nor any sign of Annie Maggio. I'll let you know if anything more develops."

He sighed in annoyance as he looked at the evening sky. The sun was almost gone now. After their run-in with Kriminel and the injury of one of his teammates, the team leader had been forced to drop him off with the medics and return immediately after he received word of the Axman's disappearance and the kidnapping of his prey.

Their current efforts felt pointless. Of course the Axman would not simply revisit his already discovered hideaway. The only reason why his Agency team was there was to potentially find any secret rooms or hovels they might have missed when they were forced out and to deal with the bodies left from the killer's massacre.

Where he should have been was with Valerie and the others, dealing with the bastard instead of now playing catch-up. He knew they had no way of knowing where and when the Axman would appear, which had been their main problem all along. But he knew about the murderer's obsession with Annie. If he felt pressured, he would only double his efforts to prevent them from rescuing her. The agent wished he knew why he wanted her so badly. It had something to do with tearing the veil down, but how would he accomplish that and what was her part to play?

"Agent Donovan!" Anderson shouted. He snapped his head to look at her and she pointed frantically at the sky. "Something is going on."

Along with almost everyone around him, he gasped in shock and disbelief. A large portal appeared over the city of New Orleans like a white tear across the sky. Several bodies fell through but he was not able to identify them from there. What followed them, however, was more terrifying than that.

A stream of spirits poured out of the portal although he couldn't tell what kind, but not all simply fell to the earth. Some began to fly and dozens headed toward his team and the wreckage of the theater. "Agents! Arm yourselves!" he ordered and retrieved his ether rifle as the spirits not only disappeared into the remains of the building but flew into the vans around them.

Why would they do that? They didn't hold any people or even interesting tech at the moment. They were merely shuttles for the—shit, the bodies. Low moans began around them and filled the air like a swarm of locusts. Burned wood from the theater was pushed aside as bodies, mangled and singed, rose from within. Screams issued from the fire fighters and paramedics as zombies lumbered out of the vans and began to grasp and claw at them as the agents opened fire.

"This is Agent Donovan! We're being attacked by zombies," he reported, blasted one through the head, and nodded when the body tumbled as the spirit erupted. "We need backup. Can anyone assist?"

"I got some guys close by," a high-pitched, accented voice replied. "I'll send them over."

"Who is this?" Donovan asked, kicked one of the zombies back, and shot it through the head.

"The name is Don Pesci. You'd best remember it, Agent."

He almost dropped his rifle. "Don Pesci? From the ghost mafia?"

"Yeah, got a problem with that?" the don asked as the car he was in swerved into the left lane. "Anyway, they'll hopefully be enough because we got our own problems over here." A loud shriek burst the windows of their spectral rides. "A banshee? Are you serious?" he grumbled as he hung up and reached for his shotgun. "Keep it steady! I'll take the bitch out."

The mob boss leaned out of the window as a dark-blue female figure flew above them. She was dressed in a tattered gown and an opaque veil obscured her features, with the exception of her wide, gaping maw. A bright light filled her lungs and he fired before she could utter another screech. The banshee rolled out of the way and wailed, and windows all around them shattered and the road beneath them broke apart.

Pesci scowled as the phantasma on his skin was torn from his ghostly form. He cursed, fired again, and caught the creature in her shoulder. The supernatural terror hissed as she fell back several car lengths.

"Yeah, how do you like that, loudmouth?" he taunted as he racked the shotgun. "Someone, take her out before—what the hell? Where did she go?" It seemed like she had disappeared over the horizon but he knew banshees were tenacious, especially when you shot them. No way would she back out now.

He squinted and tried to see if she had perhaps flown higher but was distracted by a shimmering light that illuminated the interior of his limo. He looked back and his gaze located the banshee, who was warming another cry. Quickly, he turned and prepared to fire but a loud shot preempted him and the top half of her head was blown off. She managed a stunned gasp before her body dissipated.

"You gotta be more careful, Don!" Big Daddy laughed from the car behind them and held his shotgun up. "It looked like she wanted to give you the VIP treatment."

Pesci grimaced and held his weapon up. "It don't matter. I had her grand finale right here."

"You're welcome!" the gig dealer exclaimed as he withdrew his head into the car.

The don rolled his eyes behind his shades, leaned back, and shook his head. "First the Axman gets away and now a hole in the sky is spitting out ghosts—and angry ghosts at that." He leaned his head on his fist. "What the hell is going on in this city? And where's that kid?"

CHAPTER TWO

Johnny Despereaux was used to people referring to him as "kid." He and his ghost partner detective Vic Kane stared at the massive portal in bewilderment. What had happened? They had fought Kriminel, his brother the loa Baron Samedi had appeared and captured him, and everything looked hunky-dory. Suddenly the giant skeleton body the nefarious keeper had been creating to rule both the realm of the living and the dead had exploded, and the partners fell through the supernatural gateway and landed in New Orleans.

He then realized that playing it back in his head had the sound of the ramblings of a meth head talking about the apocalypse, but it seemed to be his life at the moment.

"So…what do we do now?" he asked and looked at his partner.

"Probably get out of the way," the ghost answered. The young detective was unsure what he was talking about until he followed his gaze to a large figure that barreled down at them.

"Shit!" They both leapt to the side as the ghost landed on the roof and shook the foundation. "What? He hit the roof?" Johnny asked in bewilderment as the dust settled. "That should be only a ghost, right?"

Vic shook his head. "He's anything but 'only' a ghost kid." The lead hunter of the Wild Hunt stirred and grunted as he flattened a hand on the rooftop and pushed up.

He looked at them as a crack on his helm widened and it fell off to reveal translucent yellow skin beneath. "You—the revenant," he muttered as he stood. "What happened?"

Vic pointed at the sky. "The short version is the skeleton exploded and tore a hole between the path and living world."

"Living world?" The hunter walked past them to the edge of the roof and looked down. "No, this should not be possible." He looked skyward. "The spirits are coming back to this realm. Did you see any of my brethren among them?"

Johnny scratched the back of his head. "I was kind of out of it after the blast."

"I saw a few," the ghost detective confirmed and looked at the tops of the buildings around them. "I don't know where they landed, though."

"What of the baron?" the hunter asked. "And Kriminel?"

"I haven't seen either of them," Vic told him. "Hopefully, Samedi was able to use some of his keeper powers and get the hell out of there—preferably with his brother in tow. But I've come to learn that hoping for the best outcome is usually a fool's errand."

Johnny stepped forward. "Listen...uh, did we ever get your name?"

The ghost warrior cocked his head. "Call me Viking."

"Viking?" Vic studied him curiously. "Isn't that more of a title or position? You certainly look the part but you were named Viking?"

"No, but my birth name is of little consequence now. Even when I was alive I was not called a Viking but in modern times, most would know me as that, and that is more important to me."

"It's kind of like how Axman's real name is lost to time now, huh?" Johnny asked his partner, only to get a startled look from the ghost.

"The Axman?" Viking looked at the young man with interest. "Who is this?"

"A case we're dealing with. Don't worry about it," Vic replied quickly and pointed to the portal. "That looks far more pressing now, doesn't it?"

The hunter nodded. "Indeed. We cannot know every ghost caught in that abomination. What could be pouring out of that portal now is—Dybbuk!"

The partners instantly drew their guns as Viking brought his ax out. Above them were three ghosts who looked like they were wrapped in long cloaks with hoods and only a dark void for their faces. They reached toward them with long spindly arms and tentacle-like fingers.

"Watch yourself, Johnny. They like living hosts the best," Vic warned, but the revenant was already firing.

"Take them out before they get down here and we don't have to worry about it," he chided and blasted the malevolent spirits, who flew easily around the shots. As they drew closer, Viking dashed out in front of the partners and with a roar, swiped his ax in a violent arc that cut down all three of the terrors with one swing.

Johnny and Vic lowered their guns as the hunter placed his ax on his back.

"Much appreciated," the young detective told him.

"It is my duty, and it appears that was only a small taste of what we can expect." He scowled as he looked around. "I'm sure many of the ghosts who were trapped in that monstrosity were traumatized by their fate. If they were not already on their way to becoming terrors, then many will certainly start."

Vic tipped his hat lower. "Does that mean you'll go on one of the Wild Hunt's infamous warpaths?" he asked bluntly. Johnny questioned being so forthright with an actual hunter, but with this mess along with the Axman, they needed to know the game plan and if they could stop it.

Viking seemed to think it over for a moment. "Our numbers aren't strong enough to do so right now. I need to see how many of my comrades survived the fight and the blast. Most of the Hunt are still out on other missions, but if we cannot contain this chaos, it may come to that."

The ghost detective leaned closer to Johnny and whispered, "Fortunately, this guy doesn't seem as phantasma thirsty as the Wild Hunt are reputed to be but let's not push it. While they deal with the runaways, we need to end the Axman situation pronto."

He nodded in agreement and walked closer to Viking. "Do you think you can do anything about that portal?"

His expression regretful, the huntsman shook his head. "I am not a seer or oracle, although perhaps I can find one and see if they have any insight. But I would wager that a keeper would probably be our best hope to close it since it seems to be a tear in the path itself." He looked at him as if he'd had an idea. "See if you can find the baron. He destroyed his brother's crux, which means he should be the one to inherit Kriminel's domain."

"Find him? How?"

At a loud shriek in the distance, Viking drew his ax. "You seem to have some connection to him. I'll leave it to you to find him. I have obligations as a huntsman and I need to find my comrades." He spun and pointed his weapon at them. Johnny leaned away from the blade. "Can I trust you with this task?"

He nodded and tried to move the ax away. "Yeah, we got it, sure. You don't need to be so dramatic." Vic coughed and he added quickly, "Sir."

The hunter nodded, flew away, and disappeared behind a building. It looked like he was about to engage a terror they could not see, but if he was available to engage it, they probably didn't have to worry. They could focus on the several other things that swarmed in the back of their minds.

"All right, let's put a game plan together," Vic began. "What are our current objectives?"

"The Axman is the priority," Johnny replied and slid his hands into his jacket pockets.

The ghost looked away for a moment. "Well, yes, that's obvious, but…"

"But?" his partner prompted. "What do you mean by but? He's been the major pain in our ass the entire time we've been here, and he has Annie now."

"I know, I know. And we will get her back, but hear me out. She's probably not in any immediate danger right now. If he wanted to kill her, he already had his chance—hell, multiple chances at this point. And we don't know where he could be. I say that instead of going out on another wild goose chase while all this is going on, we should focus on finding Samedi."

"Samedi? How is that any less of a wild goose chase?" the revenant demanded and pointed at the portal. "Something must have happened to him. Otherwise, he would have dropped here with us like every other ghost. Do you have any idea where he could be?"

Vic shook his head but then pointed at his partner. "Not specifically, no, but I have an idea how we can find him."

"And how's that?"

The ghost flicked the collar of his jacket up. "Do what you did during the fight. Try to open a portal to him."

Johnny frowned. "You think it'll be that easy, huh? What about hoping for the best outcome is a fool's errand?"

"It's a long shot, sure," Vic admitted. "But it's a possibility we can at least eliminate if it doesn't work. Like Viking said, you have some kind of connection to him now. Even if it doesn't work, that might give us some indication that he...won't be an option." The implication hung in the air and the young detective folded his arms and sighed.

He had to admit, there wasn't much to lose and a whole hell of a lot to gain if it worked. If Samedi was gone in some form or fashion, though, he would hate to be the one to break the news. He nodded. "Whatever. It'll be quick."

"That's the spirit, kid." The ghost floated closer to him

before he chuckled. "Or I suppose I am, eh?" Before he could even see Johnny's eyes rolling, he fused with him and the revenant began to take his jacket off when he noticed the door to the roof. A more realistic gate or passage made a stronger crossing point.

If he intended to try it, he might as well give it the best odds. He crossed to it, slid his eyepatch up, and placed his hand on the doorknob. Unfortunately, he realized he wasn't exactly sure what he should do. Did he call out to him? Back in the path, he had simply prayed, mostly— desperate times and all that—so he settled on thinking of the loa. He turned the knob slowly before he yanked the door open to reveal a portal to Limbo, but something was off. The center glowed purple and the portal didn't provide an image of where it led.

"What do you think?" he asked warily, took a step back, and studied the crossing.

"Purple is Samedi's color," Vic replied. "We might as well see where it leads. If it's a dead-end, we can always turn back."

The revenant nodded and retrieved his phone. "Let me text Valerie and let her know we'll go looking for him." He typed the message quickly. "Hopefully, things are going all right for them."

CHAPTER THREE

"Can things get any worse?" Valerie growled as she shot a shade through its chest and it erupted into a dark fog. "We have shades, banshees, geists, and asshole ghosts and phantoms with a beef with the mafia."

"We're taking care of it," one of the mobsters assured her as he and several other members fired upon a couple of dozen other ghosts that attacked them. "We don't even know who these guys are."

"Don't you remember me, Fabio?" one of the ghosts shouted and fired a rifle shot through the mobster's hat to knock it off his skeletal head. "You and your boys took me out at the docks, remember. Reggie Allman?"

"No, I don't," Fabio shouted in return, whipped his pistol out of his suit, and fired a shot through his attacker's eye. "And if it was at the docks, you were on our turf, jackass!"

"This is why I didn't want to work with the mob." Valerie sighed as Aiyana leapt over one of the police cars and joined her. "There is always a chance you will be dragged into their bullshit."

"Well, even if we weren't, there are the terrors to contend with," the shaman reminded her as she turned to the side and blasted a shade with her flames. "The wraith has disappeared, though. Hopefully, it found other prey."

"That would be a good thing?" Valerie questioned as she reloaded.

"I do not think we are prepared to contend with a wraith at the moment," Aiyana explained. "Even with the reinforcements, they require particular abilities or rituals to deal with them effectively and we should not be focused on that for the moment. We need to find Annie."

Valerie leaned over the car and blasted a banshee in the throat as it began to scream. She stunned it but didn't obliterate it, although dozens of other shots from the agents and mafiosos finished it off. "I hate to admit it, but you are right. The supernatural division must be going crazy at the moment. We're probably the only ones making the Axman the priority right now." She looked at the shaman. "How's Marco?"

Aiyana frowned as a familiar roar sounded down the street. "Coping would be the best way to describe it, I believe."

Marco battered the shade he was fighting to pieces with his bat and turned toward one of the hostile ghosts, who pointed his revolver at him. "Hey, chill out, kid. I'm not here for you. Only the mob. Don't make me blow your brains out."

"Do you have any real bullets?" the young man asked as he approached. "Because I ain't a ghost."

The being looked at his gun. "Oh...yeah. I guess that would be a...whoa! Hey!" Marco lunged and swung his bat into the side of his skull to hurl him off the street and onto a front lawn, then through the house on the other end. At loud yells of warning, he turned to where a car was lifted into the air. He looked up at a white ghost with large, vacant eyes and an empty grin that moved it like a puppeteer.

"Watch out! Poltergeist!" an agent warned, but Marco was already running toward it. He bounded up, caught hold of the grill of the car, and hoisted himself onto the hood before he ran up it and leapt at the terror. The car dropped immediately with a loud bang and the ghost held a hand up. The young man stopped in mid-air and struggled to close the gap between him and his quarry.

Valerie stepped out from behind the vehicle and aimed. Marco lifted his bat and flung it at the geist, caught it in the face, and knocked it to the dirt. He landed, snatched his bat up quickly, and began to batter the terror so violently that it broke apart beneath him.

"That's coping?" the officer remarked as Aiyana emerged from behind their barrier.

"Perhaps blowing off steam would be better?" the shaman amended.

"They are breaking up, ladies and gents!" one of the mobsters yelled out. "Keep pushing and let's get out of this place and back to the city."

"We need to reconvene at the station—assuming anyone is there and the whole precinct isn't out dealing with all this," Valerie suggested and took a shot at a straggling shade.

"Did you see where Catherine went?" Aiyana asked and let her flames die down.

The officer nodded as she holstered her weapon. "I saw her get in a car with Big Daddy. She's safe or at least protected." She fished her phone out. "It seems like the word has gotten out—shit, Johnny went back to Limbo."

"Limbo?" Marco demanded as he stormed over. "What about my sister and the Axman?"

"He says he's going to try to find Samedi so he can close the tear in the sky and make sure Kriminel is still under lock and key." She put the phone away. "We saw the Axman lose his powers, or at least most of them. I should have asked Johnny what happened while he was gone. Something must have gone on with Kriminel."

"I did hear him scream his name as that black phantasma drained from him."

Marco rested the bat on his shoulder. "Samedi is that keeper or whatever, right? If he can find the Axman and finish him, I hope Johnny finds him soon." Anger was still clearly evident in his voice. "All right. The spooks are gone for now. What should we do?"

"We'll head to the precinct and see what is happening around the city. If we're lucky, someone might have seen the Axman while we've been dealing with this mess," Valerie told him and placed a hand on his free shoulder. "We'll find her, Marco. I promise."

He clenched his teeth but nodded solemnly. "Well, I promised to keep her safe. I hope you are better at keeping promises than I am." He wandered off and looked at the cracks still left in the street from their fight with the Axman. "Where the hell did he take you, Annie?"

When she awoke, the first thing she noticed was the smell in the air. It smelled old and rusted, but there was something sweeter as well—not flowers but some kind of plant or maybe vegetables. She shook her head and blinked a few times. When she tried to move her tired arms, she discovered that her hands were tied. She looked back to see that they were bound by coarse rope and tied to a metal grate, perhaps to a furnace. It looked old enough that it should be able to break off the wall so she tried to get to her feet and pull on it, but it wouldn't budge.

Annie sat again slowly, leaned against the wall, and tried to determine where she was. Her last memory was seeing a skeletal hand grasp her ankle and pull her into the dark. They had fought the Axman and something had happened to him. He had disappeared into a crevasse and they all thought he had escaped just when they had him. Moments later, she was taken. She looked around with wide eyes. Was this his den?

A door opened above and footsteps descended rickety stairs. Once they reached the bottom, a large white skeleton wearing dark boots and trousers riddled with holes and spectral burns walked into view.

"Axman," she said, her voice a low hiss. The murderer crossed the room with heavy steps and stared at her with flashing white lights. He leaned closer and opened his jaw, and she shrank back against the wall.

His voice was low and reverberating. "Hello, my dear key."

"Your key?" she responded and maintained as much

distance as she could despite the circumstances. "What the hell are you talking about?"

The Axman straightened, took a step back, and held a hand out. An ax manifested in it and Annie's heart began to race. He let the weapon slide through his hand until he held it by the very end and extended it to the side. Deftly, he hooked the edge of a chair and dragged it closer, then sat on it as he flipped the weapon and thunked the haft onto the floor to lean on it. "Exactly as it sounds, my dear. You are the key to all this."

"Why am I so important?" she demanded and steeled her resolve. "Why have you chased after me all this time? Why have you killed so many people and hurt my brother and friends?"

Her captor cocked his head, a glimmer in his eye. He seemed baffled by the questions. "Is that not obvious? I need you to break the veil and I needed the souls of dead victims for myself and my benefactor. Your friends—and many others—constantly got in the way."

"Your benefactor—you are talking about Kriminel."

The large skeleton nodded. "Indeed. That loa has been a pain for the last few weeks but I have to at least admit that I would not have this chance were it not for him." He raised his hand and peered at some of the wounds that remained.

"It looks like he's abandoned you now." She stared at him. "What are you? A demon?"

"Among other things," he replied. "And I don't think he abandoned me so much as he lost due to his arrogance. Trust me, I know from experience."

She jerked forward. "Then why are you still bothering?"

she demanded and tears welled in her eyes. "You've lost. It's only a matter of time before the others find you and obliterate you. Just leave!"

He chuckled wryly, leaned back in the chair, and spun the ax on the floor. "I'll admit that there has certainly been a setback, even a rather catastrophic one." He looked around the dilapidated shack or house they were in.

"It annoys me that I had to resort to coming here of all places. But despite Kriminel's confidence that nothing could stop us—or more precisely him—and that we merely needed to focus on his plan, I thought it pertinent to make a few alternatives of my own."

The killer looked at his hand again. "I always assume the worst, the better to prepare for it. If I was still connected to him and his power, we wouldn't have this conversation. I would have already begun my endgame."

"And what is that?" she asked and shifted to her knees. "What does it have to do with me and Anna Schneider?"

This seemed to get his attention and he studied her for a moment. "Circumstance, to be honest. In my life, I had no personal vendettas against my victims. Some were contracts and others were merely for fun. She was one of the survivors and on top of that, she had a child. I have to hand it to her. She was a hardy woman."

The Axman leaned forward suddenly and Annie's vision was engulfed by the glowing white light of his eyes. "If I had such a desire as simple revenge, I might have manifested as a ghoul, a dybbuk, or even a revenant, taken it, and perhaps have been destroyed by the Agency or some bounty hunter and that would have been the end of it. Fortunately for me, I wasn't so desperate and during my time in hell, I learned many interesting things—such as how truly feeble the veil between life and death is." He leaned back again and laughed. "What you are to me is not as important as what you will be, Annie. You will be the creator of my vessel—or to put it more plainly, my mother."

CHAPTER FOUR

When Johnny and Vic crossed into Limbo, they were usually ready for anything. After all, it was a land created by the memories of all its inhabitants over thousands of years on top of all the ghostly terrain, so you had to be.

But when they stepped into what appeared to be a jungle with large leaves in various shades of red, purple, and green, they were honestly somewhat taken aback. They stood in silence for a moment and stared at a sky of darkness while they heard actual animal noises that Johnny could at least suspect what they could be,

"Do you have any idea where this is?" he asked Vic, but his partner's wide, glowing eyes seemed to indicate that he was as lost as he was.

"Not a damn clue, kid. I haven't seen a place so...lifelike in Limbo." He scratched the back of his skull and adjusted his hat as he heard a screech. "Was that a monkey?"

The revenant walked to one of the trees and placed a hand on the trunk. "This kind of reminds me of the Wild Hunt's island," he pointed out. "That place seemed more detailed than normal, at least outside of the cities. Maybe this is someplace similar?"

A thought occurred to Vic and he snapped his fingers. "What if this is Samedi's place?" he suggested. "Keepers are supposed to have their palaces and whatnot. Maybe you tried to connect to him and it gave us an opening to his personal realm."

Johnny looked around. "You think? Could he be here?"

"I see a place where we can start the search," the ghost replied and pointed into the distance. "Take a look."

Johnny walked closer to him and looked at where he was pointing at large plumes of purple smoke. "It's an indication that something is here. But why would he come back?"

"Hopefully to keep his brother out of the way," Vic answered and walked down the path. "But we won't know by guessing. Stay on your guard, though. If there are monkeys, I've heard they can be vicious little bastards."

They continued along the path and a short while later, the trail turned and led them deeper into the jungle. After a few cautious steps, they reached a clearing and were shocked at what they found. The purple smoke issued from several large torches with purple flames to illuminate large gates, behind which was a massive field of graves. The ghost detective was able to push open one of them and they entered and examined the graves to discover that some were thousands of years old.

"What are all these for?" Johnny looked around and frowned at several statues of Samedi that lined the walls.

"This is probably one of Samedi's gravesites. You have to assume a guy like him would have way more than one."

Vic checked a couple of the other graves. "According to legend, Samedi is able to control whether a person lives or dies by making their grave and deciding when to fill them."

The revenant took a moment to look at the hundreds of graves. "He might be eccentric, but you can't say the guy doesn't put the work in." They walked deeper into the graveyard until they reached a plot with several open graves. "Soon to be new arrivals?"

"Most likely, or people he has deals with." They walked closer and looked at the empty burial sites. "I wonder what happens for guys like me? A half-filled grave?" He chuckled but got no reply from Johnny. He looked at him and noticed that his face was visibly pale. "What's the matter, kid?"

Johnny's pointed to the gravestone. The ghost detective moved forward quickly and the lights in his eyes dimmed. His partner's pressed lips parted and he asked, "Why has he made one for Annie?"

"Is that the last of them?" Donovan asked as he and another agent tossed one of the zombies on the pyre they had hastily constructed.

"It looks like it, sir," Coleman replied as he looked at a tablet. "But we're getting reports from across the city. All kinds of terrors and ghosts are running rampant now."

The lead agent shook his head. "Dammit. Lovett will certainly lower the dome now," he muttered and looked at the fire chief. "Do you have everything under control here?"

The man looked at the remains of the theater. "It looks like it but I wouldn't mind you leaving a couple of agents just in case. I understand if you can't."

Donovan held a hand up. "No, it's a good idea. We can't be too careful with...uh, whatever the hell that is up there." He looked at the group of ghost mafia still present but gestured to a couple of police officers who had also responded to his call for backup. "Are you gonna be all right with them?"

"Are they sticking around?"

The agent shrugged. "It's their job." He walked to the mafia, who all turned to look at him. "Thanks for your help, gentleman," he told them and made sure his rifle was aimed skyward and not at them. "So what are your plans now?"

"We'll keep moving," one of the mobsters responded and looked at his 2000s-era cell phone. "Calls and messages are coming in from everywhere. We're headed to the docks. We got a freighter that's gone silent, we need to find out why."

"You managed to get a Limbo freighter living side?" Donovan asked, almost impressed.

"Nah, it's a normal freighter manned by a living crew. It's merely under our...interests."

"Why would you tell me this?" the agent questioned.

The mafioso scoffed. "Trust me, you couldn't do nothing about it if you got all high and mighty. Besides, we're supposed to play nice for now, and we were responsible for getting the weapons." He held his phone up. "This vessel has a shipment of them, along with some other things, but I assume that's the most important thing for you and the pig...er, cops."

"Do you wanna repay the favor?" another asked. "Seeing as we helped you out of a spot, we wouldn't mind having a little help."

Donovan considered it. They did need the weapons, now more than ever, and while he wanted to report in he would probably be sent to another random area to deal with something there. He was sure Valerie and the others were still on the Axman case, and he wasn't sure when he would be able to assist. The quicker they could break up this ghost invasion and get some breathing space, the quicker he could get back to his main case, or at least do so without getting reprimanded. "Sure, we could use those weapons and we don't want any of these terrors getting out to sea."

"Yeah, it's a pain in the ass, trust me." The mobster sighed. "Get your kiddies together and follow us. By the way, you wouldn't know how to drive a boat, would you? Just in case?"

———

"Captain?" Valerie knocked and walked into Shemar's office. "What's the situation?"

Her superior officer looked at her with fatigued eyes. "It's been a hell of a week, Simone. And that was before the fucking sky blew up."

"We'll be all right, Captain. The mafia and Agency are also with us so it's not like we're facing this alone."

He laughed dryly. "I never thought I would be happy to have them around."

"Which?"

"Both." He sat at his desk and began to scroll through something on his computer. "I heard about Annie. I'm sorry she was taken but I know you'll find her."

She nodded. "She's my friend and it's my job so nothing will stop me. But that's why I've dropped by. I wanted to know if anyone reported seeing the Axman or Annie after our confrontation."

Shemar began to shake his head but stopped and stroked his chin. "You said he took her through the ground or something, right?"

"According to the people who saw her get taken. Most of us were focused on the hole he disappeared into." She frowned. If she hadn't been distracted, maybe she could have reached Annie before he did, but she shoved that thought aside. "I didn't see any tunnels or anything down there. I don't know how they traveled."

"Your report said that you were able to wound the Axman," he noted, leaned back, and folded his arms. "So he's vulnerable and potentially less powerful now, but he still has tricks." He paused and clicked a few things on his computer. "We are getting countless reports of ghosts every which way, but just before that hole in the sky appeared, we had reports of an odd light running through the streets."

"An odd light?" she questioned as he turned the monitor. "Where? Which streets?"

"I haven't had the time to put a map together," he admitted. "But a cursory look at the reports indicates that it moved out of the city. Last reports had it going northeast."

She nodded in thanks. "It's something to look into. I'll head out right away."

"All right, but before you do, you might want to check in with the big boy in the other office."

Valerie turned. "Big boy?"

"Yeah, that big purple ghost," Shemar replied. "He asked about you when he arrived. He was with a woman—a living one. He's been coordinating between the mob and our officers."

She nodded and opened the door. "So that's where he ran off to."

CHAPTER FIVE

The gravestone simply read, *Annie Maggio*. "There's no date of death," Vic muttered. "That's something of a plus, right?"

"Why did Samedi make a gravestone for her?" Johnny asked. "If he knew she was dying, wouldn't he let us know?"

His partner shook his head. "Have you not been around for our last few conversations with him? He has talked in riddles and left things out because of his rules. Maybe he can't speak about it."

The revenant sighed as he ran his fingers through his hair in frustration. "Maybe it's a good thing. You said that unless the grave is filled, they can't cross over, right? He could have made a grave so he could make sure she didn't die or something?"

Vic shrugged and began to walk away. "It's a possibility, to be sure. I have heard such stories where he staves death off for a believer for a while. Or he could have made it so she dies prematurely."

Johnny followed quickly. "Why? Can he even do that?"

"I'm not sure. It doesn't seem like something a keeper would do," the ghost admitted as they approached the exit gates at the back of the graveyard. "As for why, I would think it would probably be as a failsafe. If the Axman did get his hands on her, he could end her life before the bastard does whatever the hell he's trying to do with her."

"Would he go that far?"

Vic stopped at the gate and hung his head. "Honestly, kid, it's something I've thought of myself."

"What?" his partner asked, his voice low and shocked. "Are you kidding? You would go that far?"

The ghost turned toward him, a seriousness in his features that he was unaccustomed to despite all their years together. "I haven't told you all my stories or about all my gigs in life. One of the nice things about detective work compared to police or military is that while you make heavy decisions from time to time, they are fairly cut and dried. I can't say there were many decisions I had to make that involved massive stakes, at least not one that involved anyone beyond me and my morals. But what we are dealing with now, kid, could fuck up reality as we know it. And with stakes like that, you consider your options, especially if there's an obvious one."

"Obvious or easy?" he snapped. "You'd kill her, Vic? Or let Samedi do it? One of the basics of a job is to complete it to the best of your ability and to not stop until you've exhausted every option. Only then can you take a loss and still hold your head up."

"I know," his partner stated flatly. "I didn't say it was my go-to plan. Why do you think we're here? If we can do this in any way that doesn't end in innocent blood being spilled, even if that technically isn't an option, I'll still do my damnedest to do it. I'm only making sure you understand the stakes."

Johnny was quiet since he did unfortunately understand. As much as he balked against what Vic had said, a part of him not only grasped the plan fully but agreed with it. He hated that part. "Yeah, of course I do."

The ghost detective nodded and turned to the gate. "And to answer your question, it's obvious but if it came to the worst-case scenario, it would not be easy. We may not have known her long but Annie is a good one, and failing the good ones is never easy." He pushed the gate open and they stepped out onto the path and continued deeper into the jungle.

They proceeded in silence for a while and both detectives remained alert and watchful for any sign of possible trouble. Given their unfamiliar surroundings, they had no real idea what to expect.

"It's damn quiet," the revenant muttered and Vic nodded in agreement. They had been walking through the jungle for about ten minutes now and besides the noises they had heard before they entered, the only sounds were the foliage beneath their feet and something approximating wind. Under normal circumstances, this wasn't particularly noteworthy but in Limbo, it was very unusual.

"Should we simply keep walking?" Johnny asked, a little unsettled by the small amount of light that emanated from the trees. "I'm starting to wonder what else is here besides jungle and graves."

"This is Samedi's personal realm," Vic reminded him. "Who knows how long it stretches for?"

"That's comforting." He frowned and his steps slowed. "I'm beginning to wonder if this is worth our time. Even if we were brought here, it doesn't mean he is here. It could simply be an effect of the connection I have with him."

His partner stopped for a moment and slid his hands into his pockets. "You could be right." He looked farther down the trail and seemingly noticed something that caught his interest. "But I would imagine something has got to be here, even if he isn't." He walked a few paces farther along the path before he lowered to one knee.

"What is it?" Johnny asked and turned his attention to the jungle floor. "Do you see something?"

"It's not a clue as such…well, kind of…" The ghost held a hand up before he swiped it gingerly across the ground. After a moment, Johnny noticed large leaves under the surface layer hurried forward to help Vic to move them out of the way. They paused and stared at a large hole.

"What the hell? A pit? We're lucky to have not fallen into any of them," he exclaimed.

"It's strange, isn't it?" the ghost asked. "And right on the path too. Tell me, kid—what would a powerful keeper need basic cartoon gag traps for?"

The revenant considered it and didn't like the implications. "Do you think someone else made them? But who else could have gotten in? I know we simply made a portal but that was a special circumstance. I doubt Samedi has an open-door policy to his realm."

Vic chuckled as he pushed to his feet. "You got me there, kid, but the obvious answer is the most likely one at this point."

Johnny's face scrunched as he thought about the

obvious answer. A single name came to mind. "Kriminel? Here? I thought Samedi took care of his powers when he destroyed that big glowing orb."

"You mean his crux. That is what Samedi said, but I sure as hell don't know what a crux is. And it's not like we —" He stopped himself and focused on a tree behind them. In an instant, he drew his pistol and fired three shots into the canopy.

The young detective drew his weapon quickly, tried to see what Vic was shooting at, and jumped back when a small red body landed in front of him.

Startled, he studied the corpse and noticed its long tail. It had human-like hands and feet and when he turned it with his boot, he saw tiny ears nestled in the fur. "It's a red monkey," he said in surprise and stooped to get a better look at the creature.

"Monkeys stay together in packs or troops, I think they're called." The ghost kept his gun out as they both studied the corpse. "I guess I can't say that these monkeys would act like their living counterparts, but something still seems odd about this one."

Johnny moved one of its arms. "Have a look at this." He pointed to a large gash across its chest. "It was wounded. Do animals attack each other in Limbo?"

Vic shrugged. "Animals don't have souls. Those in Limbo were created by the memories of other ghosts— hunters who respected them or family pets held dear by the departed. I haven't heard of such a thing but I'm also not an expert." He looked warily around the jungle. "Plus, Samedi makes the rules around here, I think."

"Does this seem like any kind of animal attack you've

ever seen? Honestly, looks like a blade or something made this." He leaned closer when he noticed something inside the wound. "There's something in here, Vic."

"What? Its guts?" his partner asked and peered more pointedly at their surroundings. "I guess that wouldn't be normal for a ghost monkey."

Johnny examined it closely before he retrieved his knife and scooped something black out of it. "No, it's…phantasma."

"Phantasma? Well, if it's a ghost, it probably would have phantasma."

"No, Vic …" He stood and showed him the knife. "It's black phantasma." The familiar sludge-like substance dripped off the tip of the blade.

The ghost detective sighed. "I guess it would be too much to hope that's merely the kind of phantasma they have, huh?" Suddenly, they heard rushing sounds behind the trees. Johnny held his knife up beneath his gun as they stood back to back. Figures began to emerge from within the vegetation and they both tensed.

He had a look at one of them, although it did him little good. It resembled a person dressed in dark robes and pants but he could not see its face and its arms looked wrong. They were skeletal with a dark coating of some kind of dust or fog.

One of them held the corpse of a bird and tossed it aside. Another emerged from the jungle floor. It stretched up with both hands, curved them at a frightening angle to bend back and place them on the ground, and pushed itself up. It hobbled forward, its head obscured by the hood of the robe, and raised its head slowly to look at the others.

The face was skeletal but oddly so, like the flesh was still there but folded in and turned to bone. Etchings traced along its brow and its teeth had been sharpened.

"Vic? What the hell are these?" Johnny asked, his voice low and almost a whisper as he turned the power of his gun up slightly.

"They are called shadows. Shades with a little more meat on them—figuratively, at least." Two more dropped from above. A chill ran through the revenant's body and he looked down at an odd bump on the path. He grabbed Vic and jumped out of the way as two beings thrust from the dirt and faced them, one holding a machete.

"Well, there's a shitload of them," he muttered. "And you said they were like shades, huh?"

The ghost nodded. "And who do you know who's fond of shades?"

Johnny sighed and shook his head as he aimed at one of the shadows. "Kriminel."

CHAPTER SIX

"Big Daddy?" Valerie called as she stepped into the office alongside Aiyana and Marco.

The ghost in question looked at her from behind the desk where he was seated, a phone pressed against the side of his head. "Ah, it's good to see you came back." He glanced at Catherine, who sat in a chair reading a book. "I told you they would be all right."

She looked up from her tome and smiled. "It's good to see you again."

"Seriously? The last time you saw us the Axman appeared," the officer pointed out.

The woman frowned slightly and shrugged as she closed her book. "That's true, I guess, but it is nice to see you safe."

"And the same to you," Aiyana told her.

Valerie folded her arms and looked at Big Daddy. "The chief said you wanted to see me."

The ghost put his phone down. "Yes but no. I was

looking for Johnny but I hoped you could put me in touch if he didn't arrive. I can't seem to get hold of him."

She frowned. "That's because he's not here—and I'm not talking about being in New Orleans."

"What? Is he in Limbo?" He pointed the phone at her. "That's not a problem for me. I've got the deluxe package. I can reach anyone on either side with this baby."

Baffled, she stared at the phone. "How does that even work?" She waved dismissively. "You know what? It doesn't matter. You probably can't reach him because he's busy." She took her phone out and opened her texts. "He said he was going after Samedi."

"Samedi?" Big Daddy looked at the device and Catherine perked up. "Going after him where?"

The officer shrugged. "I don't know. He said he was trying to find him after they were separated during the fight with Kriminel."

"They fought Kriminel?" Catherine gasped. "If that is so, perhaps it has something to do with the anomaly in the sky."

The ghost dealer chuckled. "Yeah, a fight between two keepers would do that." He sighed and leaned back. "So we have no way to reach him?"

"You would have a better chance of that than I would," Valerie pointed out.

Catherine held a hand up. "I might be able to," she offered and caught their attention. "Well, I might be able to contact Samedi, which would eventually get to Johnny." She dug in her purse and brought out several objects, including candles and a photo. "I can cross over as a spirit and perhaps make contact with the loa."

"On your own?" Big Daddy stood from his chair. "Let me go with you, Cathie."

She waved him off as she sat on the floor and positioned the objects around her. "I'll be fine, Marsan. You worry too much. It is not like I'm looking for a demon or anything. Besides, you wouldn't be able to come with me anyway since you are a ghost." She paused and looked at the group. "But perhaps you would like to?"

"Do what?" Valerie asked.

Aiyana answered for her. "Go with her. It would appear she is preparing a ritual that would allow her to go into the spirit realm. I believe you would be most familiar with it as astral projection."

Catherine nodded. "Yes, indeed. Others can join me but they need to be living." She smiled at the ghost. "Those are simply the rules, Marsan." He grumbled in response and leaned back in the chair.

"Is it dangerous?" the officer asked.

The priestess frowned. "It can be if something goes wrong. I am trying to make contact with a loa and even with my skill, it depends if he is open or not. But if he's not, it is more likely that nothing at all will happen. But going in alone can be intimidating."

The other two women looked at one another and seemed to have made their minds up. When they looked at Marco, he shook his head. "Hell no, but hurry back so we can continue to look for my sister, all right?"

Valerie nodded to him. "Sure thing, but don't go anywhere without us." She sat on the floor next to Catherine and Aiyana sat across from her. "All right, what do we have to do?"

The voodoo priestess extended an arm to either side, lit a candle, and placed it in her mouth. "Take each other's hands. Close your eyes and free your mind," she said around the candle. "Don't fight the pull once you feel it. I shall begin and hope Samedi answers."

She closed her eyes and the other women followed suit.

At first, she merely hummed before she spoke in a language Valerie had heard before but was not familiar with—Haitian maybe? The officer lowered her head and felt nothing, but she heard the chants. A short while later, she felt like she was being lifted and listened to Catherine's advice and let it happen, although she could not help the mixture of unease and excitement that accompanied the experience. She saw a light that turned to shades of purple, pink, blue, and black and she seemed to soar through it toward something that came up fast in the distance.

The three women plummeted suddenly to land on something surprisingly soft. The priestess was prepared for concrete or maybe even a never-ending void. She preferred to not have the latter, but when she went through a supernatural gate and had no idea of what was on the other side, she tended to get imaginative.

"Are you both all right?" she asked, pushed up, and dusted her dress. She looked back to where Valerie had offered a hand to the shaman to help her up. It seemed to have gone limp, however, and Aiyana mostly used it for support as she stood slowly.

Catherine looked at the officer, who gazed at something in awe. The sky behind the woman was pitch black and when she turned to look at what Valerie was staring at, she was met with more darkness. Small glimmers of light were scattered across it and resembled a night sky, but it was too ebon. This was some kind of abyss.

Surprisingly, she could see everything clearly, although the lighting was odd and everything had an unnatural purple hue. She looked at her hands, then lowered her gaze to focus on what they had landed on—a field of purple... something, maybe grass—that rolled into itself, all burrowed into the dirt. She bent and touched it tentatively. It was soft, akin to cotton, and shimmered with a luminescence much like the trees. At least a dozen of them with dark-blue trunks were planted in the field. Pink petals drifted off them to color the ground and sky with soft hues.

"This is...oddly pleasant." Valerie finally snapped out of her blank stare.

"Where...where are we?" Aiyana asked and looked at the mystical field in bemusement. "Is this where the baron lives?"

The priestess scanned their surroundings. She had made contact with the loa on a few rare occasions during her life, but this wasn't what she remembered. Her memory conjured the recollection of a jungle with decorations and buildings that looked like they would be at home in Haiti or Africa. "Perhaps this is his summer home," she suggested, mostly to herself. She took a few steps and placed her hands on her hips as her gaze swept around her again. "It is quite something, isn't it?"

"I won't disagree. These...uh, plants feel quite nice." Aiyana let her feet glide over the soft purple grass.

"I feel like that sky could swallow me whole," Valerie remarked and folded her arms. "So this is what the other side is like, huh? I guess I can't fault the ghosts for trying to return to somewhere normal."

"In time, Limbo will be more normal for them than Earth would be," Catherine told her. "So do either of you see a castle?" she asked and turned to her companions. She was going off what she remembered, even if it wasn't exactly this. But she did recall that Samedi lived in a palace or a mansion with ornate decorations and graves surrounding the fields.

"I don't see any castle." The officer took a few steps forward and pointed up a hill in the distance. "I think that's a house, though."

The priestess turned and peered into the distance. There was indeed a house—a rather quaint, single-story building with white walls, a black arched roof, and a nice little fence painted black with pink dots to match the petals of the trees.

She wondered if she had made some kind of mistake during the ritual as she turned slowly to look at the other women. Her smile remained but she wondered what they were thinking. "It is...um, rather nice, is it not?"

"I suppose so. But are you sure we are in Samedi's domain?" Aiyana asked and her brows furrowed quizzically.

Catherine was questioning that herself. "We would not be pulled anywhere else," she replied and began to walk in the direction of the house. "We would not be pulled anywhere else other than where he—"

"Ah, well, who do we have here?" A deep, yet somewhat soothing and even a tad whimsical voice drifted into her mind. She turned again and the shock on both Aiyana and Valerie's faces confirmed that they had heard it too.

"That wasn't one of you, was it?" the officer asked. Both shook their heads and when they looked up, Aiyana stumbled back and fell while Valerie's trance-like gaze returned. Both looked at something behind their companion.

"I must say, it is quite lucky for me that one of my followers is so gifted." Something touched one of the priestess' shoulders, then the other, and gave them a light squeeze. "In my current condition, not many would have been able to call out to me. Especially so clearly."

She turned slowly and saw nothing but more darkness since a black suit loomed in front of her. Her gaze drifted to what was a rather off-putting visage. It was a skull or at least shaped like one. The face peered at her with purple irises set in glowing white eyes and the entire head was caked in clay or thick make-up that gave it a heftier look.

It was painted and wore a large, wide-brimmed hat, although half of it looked like it had been ripped apart. When she backed away slightly, she noticed that the suit was damaged as well. A large chunk of what would be a rib cage was missing and purple light flowed out.

When she looked at the face again, it wore an eerie smile exaggerated by more black paint that covered the entire bottom half of his face. Purple lines cut across from one eye to the other and intersected with the black line. This otherworldly being cocked its head and took a moment to look from her to the others before it returned its focus to her. "So I have allowed you to find me. Do you think yourself worthy?"

"Worthy?" she asked and her eyes widened. "Baron Samedi?"

He laughed hoarsely at her utter astonishment, backed away to bow, and coughed as he straightened again. "Indeed, my dear priestess. I'm glad you came." He staggered for a moment and fell back, and Catherine hurried forward to help him. "And the worthy question was only a joke, child. I'm in need of your aid."

CHAPTER SEVEN

"Can I help you?" the boat captain asked. His three-man crew stared curiously as Donovan, his team, and the ghost mafia approached.

"My name is Agent Donovan and I'm with the SEA," he stated as he retrieved his ID and held it up. "We need to commandeer this boat to investigate a possible supernatural situation out at sea."

The man leaned against the wall. "Is that right?" He tilted his head slightly. "The SEA? Ain't that fitting? Are these guys with you, Rick?"

The mafioso behind the lead agent chuckled and trudged forward with a slight nod. "They are, Bobby. As you can probably tell, things are a little freaky at the moment."

"It's not a surprise with that gaping hole in the sky." The captain chuckled, extended his hand, and took Rick's in a firm shake. "But is it so bad that you've teamed up with the Agency?"

"Do we look thrilled about it either?" Coleman mumbled under his breath.

Rick looked back and shrugged. "All of us are only trying to get things back nice and tidy in a quick fashion, you know? We're here 'cause we need to see what the hell is going on with the shipment."

"The freighter?" Bobby asked and the ghost nodded. "Yeah, some of the guys working the pier asked about it. We haven't had a chance to head out to sea yet—you know, with that weird-ass thing up there taking all our attention."

The mobster looked out into the bay. "So it should be clear for the most part, then?"

"Of other fishing boats and smaller commercial boats, yeah." The captain turned and pointed at the darkened sky. "It looks like rain, or at least that's what I would think if it wasn't for the weirdness. But beyond that, we got a fog settling in."

"Is it safe to go out in those conditions?" an agent asked.

Bobby and his men chuckled in his response. "Well, it ain't a sunny day, but something like that ain't gonna kill you unless you ain't got any sea legs. Do those not come standard for SEA agents?"

Donovan stepped forward. "We'll be fine. But can you get us to the freighter?"

"Of course I can," he said confidently. "The real question is if something is on that boat, can you take care of it? It's not like me and my boys spend the off-season hunting ghosts ourselves."

Rick placed a comforting hand on the captain's shoulder. "No need to worry there, Bob. Me and the boys are gonna comb through and exorcise that big bastard of a boat. You know that no one fucks with the mob and gets away with it, even if they are only mindless terrors." He thumbed at the agents. "And these guys can handle themselves. It turns out those shiny weapons of theirs are good for something."

The captain nodded and motioned to one of his men, who dropped a large piece of wood onto the dock. "All right then. Get on board and let's head out. I'd prefer to deal with this sooner rather than later and get these spooks out of our waters. No offense to you and the rest, Rick."

His mafia friend merely chuckled. "It's all good, Bobby. I want them gone too. It hurts business." He turned and pointed to his gang. "Get on board, all of you. If you have any spare stygia, suck it down and be ready to board the freighter." He removed his hat and bowed dramatically to Donovan. "And, of course, I should welcome the SEA aboard."

Bobby smirked and saluted the agents as they and the ghosts filed quickly on board. Donovan approached him, his expression curious. "This is a sizeable vessel but you only have a crew of three and yourself?"

The man's smirk widened. "Well, we have a few more men who didn't show up this morning. I guess it's not surprising given everything, you know? But as far as a crew of three goes, that's only technically right." he turned and shouted, "Sully! Thomas! Get out here and greet the new arrivals."

Two ghosts appeared a moment later. The green one wore a sleeveless tank top, a red beanie, and long trousers that displayed his skeletal arms and feet. The other was blue and dressed in a long jacket, a striped shirt, and slacks.

He had a curled mustache and drank from a mug. "Aye, captain?" the green one asked.

"You have ghosts in your crew?" Donovan asked in astonishment.

Bobby nodded. "I certainly ain't afraid to work with ghosts. Hell, they technically have more experience at sea than I do although they aren't used to modern technology." The ghosts approached him and he clapped the blue one on the shoulder. "Sully here is the real captain. I'm only called that for appearances."

"I'm the better navigator and helmsman, Bobby," he replied with an Irish drawl as he sipped from his cup. "Besides, this is your vessel. If I start calling it mine, I'll have to pay for the upkeep."

"Are you drinking stygian coffee?" the agent asked.

Sully lifted the mug to his teeth and took a long sip while he nodded. "It's great stuff. We have to be a little more careful with our use of stygia out at sea. I'd offer you some but it does some nasty stuff to breathers." He knocked the back of his hand against the other ghost. "Go and help the others get this boat going, Thomas."

"I'm on it." The green ghost nodded and darted away to help one of the other crewmen unwind the ropes.

"Did he drink the coffee too?" Donovan asked when he noticed how quickly the ghost worked. "He's certainly got some pep in his step."

Bobby and Sully chuckled and the ghost shook his head. "Not really. From time to time, perhaps, but he's got his own preference." Almost as if to prove his point, the ghost took a flask out quickly, popped the top and took a swig, then capped it and replaced it in his back pocket.

"Have we got a destination, Captain?" Sully asked when he turned his mug upside down and confirmed that it was empty.

"Indeed we do, Captain," Bobby answered and nodded to Rick. "Our friend Rick here needs to go check on one of his shipments out at sea. He'll give you the coordinates."

The mobster took his phone out. "I got them right here. Are we ready to go?"

Sully and Bobby looked at their men. One caught their glances, nodded, and gave them a thumbs-up. "It seems we are," the captain replied.

"Then let's begin," Sully stated briskly as they both headed into the cockpit. "After I pour myself a fresh cup."

The shadow with the machete lurched forward and waved its blade wildly in the air. The partners fired at it at the same time and two holes appeared in its chest. It fell back for a moment before it stirred and pushed to its feet.

"What the hell? It took an ether and spectral shot to the chest," Johnny shouted. "How do we deal with these bastards?"

Vic fired several more shots—three to the chest, one to the stomach, and two to the head. The shadow fell back again and exploded into dark dust. "You shoot them as many times as it takes," he responded and glowered at the dozen or so shadows still present. "Be careful to not focus on one too much and make sure you don't overload your gun. These only want to kill. They don't play with their food."

"Are you saying they eat people?" Johnny questioned as he stood back to back with Vic and focused on the four shadows approaching him while he kept an eye on the three to his side.

The ghost detective pulled the hammer back on his gun. "I don't think that's what they are trying to do necessarily, but they can be somewhat barbaric." He fired quickly when one of the shadows surged forward and blasted it in the head. It fell back and another ran forward. "You know what? It's best to not find out." He fired on the approaching shadows before he was forced to leap to the side to dodge one that pushed through from below.

Johnny used the opposite tactic and ran toward them. They attempted to strike at him but he jumped and fired a maximum charged shot down to hurl them all back and launch himself higher. He was able to land behind them before he turned and fired at the group again. The power of the shot made him slide back and into a tree but it blasted the top half off one of them and the arm and part of the head of another.

He steadied himself on the tree and aimed before he felt a sudden pain in his arm. With a gasp, he clutched it as he turned toward a shadow with enlarged claws that stood close to him. "How the hell did you get there?" He growled in annoyance as it dove in for another strike, but he yanked his knife out and shoved the claws away.

The young detective dug the blade into its stomach and dragged it through the side. He turned the power on his gun down, jammed it into the tear, and fired to blast the being's abdomen to shreds. What remained of the body slumped and dissolved.

When he looked back, the shadow with the partially destroyed head lunged toward him. He slammed his blade into the underside of its jaw, twirled it, and placed his gun barrel on the top of its head for a kill shot. Before he could fire, another entity wielding a blade lurched forward and swiped wildly. Johnny used the shadow he had in his grasp to defend against the blows before he kicked it off his knife and into the other one and fired several shots through both.

Vic had managed to get one of them under his boot and fired three shots into its head to destroy it. He turned as two shadows advanced on him, leaping through the trees. "Oh, come on now, that's ridiculous," he muttered.

He flipped his jacket open and reached to a box on his belt, opened it, and withdrew a bullet with a swirling mass of ether in the tip. With a grim smile, he loaded it into his revolver and aimed between them.

"Sorry, guys. I don't have time to choose favorites." He fired the bullet and followed it immediately with a spectral shot. Ether did not react well with phantasma, which was the point. When the spectral shot passed through the bullet and hit the ether, it erupted into a blast that engulfed both shadows before they disintegrated.

Movement caught his attention and he looked down at a dark hump in the dirt that traveled quickly toward him. He accessed the bullet box on his belt again and chose a silver bullet with a bright orange tip.

"Oh, I've got something for your ass," he muttered, loaded it, and jumped back to fire in front of the hump. The bullet struck the dirt and erupted into ecto flames. The shadow burst from the ground and was caught in the supernatural fire. Its eyes darkened as it began to melt and he aimed with his revolver and fired a shot through its head. It fell to its knees and the flames consumed it.

The ghost detective removed his hat and rubbed his skull. "That certainly wasn't pretty," he commented and grimaced as the flames began to spread to some of the trees. "Huh. I hope Samedi isn't too peeved about that."

When he heard a shout in the distance, he donned his hat hastily. It could only be Johnny. They probably shouldn't have split up but fortunately, they were never too far from one another. He turned translucent and darted toward his partner as if to fuse.

The young detective fought with a shadow that tried to bury a hatchet into his head. Vic fused with him for only a moment before he thrust out and drove a fist into the shadow's face to knock it away. Johnny snatched up his gun that had been dislodged from his grasp, turned it to maximum, and fired a shot that obliterated the being. The force launched him into a slide and he had barely enough time to shield his head before he bulldozed into a tree.

"Are you all right, kid?" Vic asked as his partner cursed under his breath and pushed to his feet.

Johnny rolled his shoulders and felt his head with his free hand. "It looks like my pride was hurt more than anything," he muttered before he checked his arm. "Well, this too, I guess."

"You got nicked?" The ghost examined the injury. He stepped back and pushed the sleeve on his coat up to reveal a small scratch on his arm. "Huh. I didn't feel a thing."

The revenant looked at the mark and grimaced. "Sorry. I should have kept better track of my surroundings."

He let his sleeve fall. "Don't beat yourself up now, kid. It ain't a big deal. You're the one with the real injury."

His partner shrugged. "I got about eight. What about you?"

Vic looked at him and made a mental tally. "Six in all. Including the one we both shot and I finished off."

"We don't both get to count that one?"

The ghost shook his head. "Nah, killing shots only. That's always been the rules."

Johnny sighed and holstered his gun. "Fine. I guess I got seven then. It's still higher than yours."

"Despite the help you needed with the last one?"

He rolled his eyes. "I could've handled it. I still had my knife too..." He slid his hand to his belt but his knife was missing from its sheath.

Vic held it up. "Are you looking for something, partner?"

The young detective grunted as he took it and put it in its sheath. "We can argue who won later. What's the next move? We need to decide whether to push forward and look for the baron or head back and help in New Orleans."

His partner looked around the jungle. "Well, I think running into those shadows indicates one thing."

"That Kriminel could be here, right?" Johnny scratched his head. "I suppose it's possible. But we also thought Samedi would be here and we have seen neither hair nor hide of him yet. This place was eerie enough to walk through looking for someone who likes us. I don't think it will be much better looking for someone who seriously wants to kill us."

"I think killing us would be a mercy if we somehow

fuck up and he gets hold of us," Vic told him but rubbed his chin thoughtfully. "Still, he is weaker now. If we have the opportunity to finish him, we should probably take it."

"Do we even have the firepower to do that?" the young man asked. "I didn't exactly bring any ether bombs with me. We are technically bounty hunters but that's merely semantics. We don't usually take the jobs that require us to kill big nasty things."

"I don't think he is anymore. You remember what he looked like before the skeleton exploded."

Johnny thought back and nodded. "He looked frail and shrunken. Although he was still bigger than you or me it was only by a couple of feet. Samedi looked like he could stomp on him and end it."

"I wish he had," the ghost replied bitterly. "Personally, if we can end him, I would rather do that than have him still in the game. Valerie said something happened to the Axman, right? Their connection was probably severed but if Kriminel gets back to him, that means trouble."

"Maybe he's trapped here somehow," the revenant suggested. "After Samedi took his…that, uh…"

"The crux?"

"Right, that." He snapped his fingers. "What is that? You seem to know something about it."

Vic folded his arms. "I've mostly pieced things together based on what I've heard and what Samedi said. Think of it as kind of a secondary soul for a keeper. It allows them all their powers and abilities—or more powerful versions of them at least." He kicked the dirt. "Although if that was him, it still seems like he can summon shades and shadows."

"Right, but he doesn't have it now." Johnny gestured around him. "He probably had a place like this but can't access it."

"So he ended up trapped here?" his partner muttered. "I guess we're speaking hypothetically, but even with his crux destroyed, his connection to his brother probably still remained. It's risky to go to his domain, though, but if he did, he must have some kind of plan."

"Either that or no other option." The revenant looked puzzled and peered deeper into the jungle. "Shit. You might be right. Maybe he didn't try to go to New Orleans to get the Axman's help because he couldn't or can't in some way. He can't come and go as he pleases and he knows a hell of a lot of people are looking for him now in the land of the living."

"So you also think we should take him out?"

Johnny sighed. "I'm still stuck on can we?"

Vic looked at his gun. "I think of it like this. We still have to find the bastard or Samedi. The best-case scenario is we find Samedi and together, we find Kriminel and obliterate the jackass. And the worst-case is we find nothing and we wasted our time."

The young man frowned. "Given the circumstances, that could be a very bad thing with everything going on in New Orleans."

Vic nodded. "True, but I have a hard time believing that will happen."

"Why's that?"

"Because if there wasn't something to bring us here or someone to guide us, how the hell did we get here?"

Johnny did not have an answer for that. "Fine. That's a

decent point. But I say that unless we find something extremely odd in the next couple of hours, we need to return to New Orleans before we try anything else." He was interrupted when a blast of purple light appeared in front of them. It coalesced into the form of a woman wearing a top hat. "What the hell?"

The ghost shielded his lights before he looked at him. "Do you think this qualifies?"

CHAPTER EIGHT

Don Pesci burst through the large double doors of the front of the warehouse and walked into the middle of the large space, where several mafia members waited for him beside a large desk.

"Greetings, Don Pesci." One of them gestured to the desk. "Sorry about the accommodations. This was the best we could do on such short—"

"It's fine. I'm not here to kick back." The mob boss cut him off and one of his bodyguards pulled the chair back as he sat and tossed the suitcase he carried onto the desk. He took a cigar from his jacket pocket and lit it before he looked at the gathered men with a trace of irritation. "All right, what do you mooks want? I'm not sure if you've noticed, but hell is peeking through a crack in the door and you thought now was a good time for a get-together?"

The capos all stared at him or each other before one in a red dress suit stepped forward. "Uh…sorry, sir, but we were told to meet you here. At least…I was told that you wanted to see us."

"Do what?" Pesci scowled as the others murmured agreement. "I didn't put a call out. I was busy in the streets where you and your men should be."

"There's no need to be so pissy, Pesci," a dark voice croaked. The capos looked around wildly as some of them and the bodyguards drew their weapons.

The don, however, gazed casually around the warehouse. "So you finally decided to get your miserable undeath over with, huh?" He popped the case open and took a drag of his cigar. "I've been waiting to get face to face with your ugly mug."

A loud cackle preceded the response. "I admire your bravado. I guess you would grow quite a backbone being the head of the ghost mafia."

He snarled. "I don't need to be brave to deal with you. The only time I got a good look at you was when you were crawling on the pavement getting blasted to hell. It's a pity it didn't take." He reached into the case, pulled his shotgun out, and racked it as he turned in his chair.

"It was something of a setback, admittedly." Although it seemed like he tried to stay calm, an irate tone crept into the Axman's voice. "But one I hoped you could assist me with."

"I ain't doing shit for you!" Pesci roared and stood from his chair. "What I will do is obliterate you and piss on whatever remains while I'm at it. Now get the hell out here, you miserable fuck!" He'd barely finished speaking when two bodyguards fell, each with a hatchet in their chest.

"Don, look out!" one of the capos warned. The mob

boss looked into the dark and ducked as a larger ax was flung over his head. It thunked into the desk and slid it toward the capos in front of it. Some jumped out of the way while others went intangible and it continued past them, flipped, and landed heavily. The ax embedded in it shook before it yanked itself out of the wood and hurtled toward Pesci, who kept his head down as it sailed overhead and landed in the skeletal palm of the Axman.

The don scrambled quickly to his feet and aimed his shotgun. "You seriously are nothing but a bag of bones, aren't ya?" He sneered and fired a shot. His adversary blocked some of the spectral pellets with his ax but the spread meant that some were able to hit him in the shoulder and side of his head.

He racked his shotgun. "Are you simply gonna stand there? Go ahead, you freak. Make it easy for me!" Pesci took a moment to look at the capos. "Would you guys get in here and help me waste this son of a bitch?"

Something pulled at his gun and he spun quickly. The intruder was now directly in front of him and yanked the gun up and the mafioso along with it.

Before he could react, the Axman released the weapon and grasped him by the collar of his suit. He turned and thrust him against a pillar as he hooked his ax into his belt and raised his hand. Black phantasma coated the skeletal fingertips.

"You are quite right, Don. I am not the same Axman you've heard about." He placed his fingers against Pesci's skull. "Because of that keeper's idiocy, he failed his end of the arrangement but I have prepared for such a problem. I merely need the phantasma to make it work." Pesci whimpered as the color began to fade from his bones. "And longstanding members of the ghost mob like yourself and your associates should be able to give me the souls I need to—"

Suddenly, several ghostly vehicles appeared in the warehouse.

The Axman was surprised by their arrival and number. His captive used the moment of distraction, flicked his wrist, and a switchblade dropped into his hand.

"You were alone!" the killer protested. "Where did they come from?"

"I'm the don, dumbass!" Pesci growled, opened the blade, and readied it as his attacker turned his head toward him. "Do you think I ain't bonded with my trusted soldiers? They know when I need them!"

He dug the blade into the Axman's eye—normally a pointless action, but this was a stygian blade coated in ether and damaging to the living and dead alike. This fortunately included his assailant, who hissed in pain as his hold slackened enough for the don to kick off him and out of his grasp. The Axman ripped the blade out of his eye socket, turned, and faced the horde of mobsters who poured out of the vehicles.

The mob boss rolled on the floor and snatched his shotgun along the way. "What are you mooks waiting for? Blast him!" he ordered and they all began to fire. Their target drew his ax and knocked away some of the shots but was bombarded with spectral rounds by the entire group. He screamed with rage and slammed his ax into the ground to create a fissure large enough for a couple of the cars along with some of the mafia members to be sucked in. While the men scrambled away from the large crevasse, he pointed to the desk and it began to glow.

"Don! Some kind of sigil is on the bottom of the—" The capo didn't get to finish as a torrent of shades appeared. Two caught hold of him and lifted him, and he shrieked as he was ripped in two. As the mafia were now distracted by the shades, the Axman moved decisively toward Pesci, who saw him coming. He walked back and fired a couple of rounds into his adversary before he jumped onto one of the cars, ghosted through the window, and accelerated sharply as he drove it straight toward his opponent.

The serial killer stood firm and looked like he attempted to catch the car when it ran into him, but the mob boss kept his foot flat on the gas pedal and rammed him. The light in the Axman's good eye flared as he was caught on the front of the car and it crushed his ribs. Pesci braked sharply to dislodge him and readied his shotgun while his now recovered bodyguards joined him along with a few other mafiosos to check on the prone figure. The don aimed, his features set in a scowl. "Hold up. I'll end this prick," he ordered and prepared to fire.

Without warning, the Axman bounded to his feet and leapt on the don to hurl him to the floor. He raised his hand with the black phantasma and attempted to take Pesci's soul but one of the bodyguards managed to kick him off. The killer rolled along the floor and held his jaw where he had been hit to stop it from falling open. He had been kicked and it had worked because he felt pain.

As he'd expected, all the mob members now aimed at

him. He whisked a hand forward and several shades swooped in response. The don saw them in time and his men all turned to fire. They were able to destroy them but the distraction gave the Axman enough time to create another, smaller fissure. It was barely big enough for him to squeeze into and disappear to Limbo.

A rage built inside him. He had lost his victim and he'd had a fresh reminder of how weak he was now. It would not be for long, he promised himself. He was too close to getting everything he wanted.

"Freighter in sight, sir!" Thomas shouted as the large boat loomed ahead of them as a rather dark image obscured by the fog.

"Come about!" Bobby ordered and looked at Rick and Donovan. "Is this your haunted freighter?"

The mobster looked at his phone. "It looks like it. The coordinates are a little off but it probably drifted between when I got them and now."

"I'll get my team ready." The agent turned to leave but stopped and looked over his shoulder. "Did you ever get any response on what exactly we can expect to deal with?"

Rick flicked through his phone. "I got some blurry images—oh, wait. There's a video here." Donovan stepped back as he, Rick, Bobby, and Sully all looked at the screen. When the video started, a sweaty, terrified crewman looked into the camera with wide eyes.

"Hey, you need to get people over here!" he hollered and screams and shouts could be heard in the background.

"Something is here. The guards are all dead and obliterated. Whatever these things are swallowed them and turned them into ash and now, they are attacking the living crewmen and— It's everywhere, man! There are blood and bodies…you need to get here!"

"Swallowed?" Rick asked, cocked his head, and glanced at Donovan. "What terror swallows people?"

"There are a few possibilities but out here in the ocean, the most likely would be a siren or ocean wraith," the agent replied.

Bobby looked at him, his expression perplexed. "Sirens are real?"

The man raised a hand and shook it from side to side. "They aren't the enchanting beauties who will run your boat into rocks with song. That's merely what we call them. They are typically female ghosts similar to banshees who died tragically in the water. It could be the sea or even a bathtub. What interests me is whatever turned them to ash. I'm not entirely sure what that could be, but he could merely be describing it the best way he knows how, not what it is doing." He looked at Rick. "Either way, if you brought anything special with you, I'd bust it out."

"That was already the plan," the mobster replied and nodded to the phone. "There are a few seconds left."

When he hit the play button, the crewman on the screen turned and paled. He screamed and held his hands up as what appeared to be a liquid enveloped his arms and head and dragged him away. His screams continued but they were muffled, and a few moments later, they could hear choked gasps.

Two other crewmen ran in and yelled for him and

pulled at something before they both lost their grasp and he went completely silent. One told the other they had to go, noticed the camera, and typed something quickly before he ended the stream.

The four stood in silence for a short while and Sully was the first to speak. "That...uh, is that normal for a siren?"

Donovan looked at him with dull eyes and shook his head. "No, not at all. It looks like we're dealing with a drowned."

"Drowned?" Rick frowned as he put his phone away. "I've never heard of them."

The agent paused to consider his words. "I guess you could say they are like water-based zombies or ghouls. Their bodies are made of phantasma, seawater, and digestive acids. They eat their victims like zombies or ghouls do but instead of tearing chunks out of them, they absorb them and drain them until they look like mush. This is then added to their bodies and increases their strength and durability outside water."

All of them grimaced. The mobster looked up at the freighter as the crewman threw grappling hooks onto the rails above. "Do they...uh, go after ghosts too?"

Donovan nodded. "Yeah, they are ghosts themselves and a good chunk of their form is made of phantasma. If they pull you in, you are as screwed as I would be."

Rick considered this for a moment and shuddered slightly as he looked at Bobby. "Hey, Bob. You wouldn't still happen to have that stash we gave you, would you?"

The captain nodded. "We haven't had a use for it yet. It's down in the stash area where we left it."

"Good. We'll probably need that. We brought our normal guns and this is looking like a special situation in need of special goods."

"No problem." Bobby reached over and got on the horn. "Thomas, Victor! I need you to guide Rick to the stash area. He'll need something with a little more kick to it." The ghost and his crewmate acknowledged the order.

Rick began to leave the cockpit and Donovan looked at him. "We'll head up while you're getting prepared and get a layout."

The ghost nodded and cast a dark glance at the large vessel. "We'll be up soon and I guess we'll take the direction you guys don't."

"That sounds good to me. We'll take the front of the boat."

"Fine by me." The mobster nodded.

Donovan dug in a pouch on his belt and withdrew a small circular device. "Here's a comm. It links directly to me in case you need to report."

Rick took the device and flipped it between his fingers before he placed it in his jacket pocket. "All right. And if you see anything, scream. We'll get the picture."

He left and the agent prepared to follow when a large hand settled on his shoulder. "Are you sure don't want to take a look at the stock?" the captain asked. "I'm sure the SEA has some nice toys but it couldn't hurt to have a little something extra, savvy?"

Donovan smirked. "Trust me, we'll be fine. We're a little more prepared than our new colleagues are for this kind of thing." He turned and grasped the handle of the door to the cockpit. "You don't need to worry about us. This is our job.

We're professional, and we don't scream." With that, he shut the cockpit door and gathered his team as the mafia members headed into the boat. He felt a splash on his head, looked up, and scowled when he realized it had begun to drizzle now. "Do we have wet gear?" he called.

"Right here, sir!" one of the agents responded, brought a large case forward, and placed it on the deck.

"Thanks, Franco." The team leader stripped his jacket off. "Look here, ladies and gentleman, I can only confirm that there are drowned onboard. That said, it seems there could be a few different types of terrors and we do not know how many there currently are. Until we can assess that, we stick together and keep weapons hot. There might be survivors to look out for but our priority is to eliminate the terrors. It's no good rescuing anyone if they are still in a haunted ship, all right?"

"Yes, sir!" they all replied as they removed their jackets and replaced them with a wetsuit-like slicker and boots with rubber grips.

Once Donovan had changed and slid his Agency pack on, he took hold of one of the ropes, thanked the crewman, and climbed quickly onto the boat. When he landed on the deck, he immediately drew his rifle and shortened the barrel.

A light popped out of the shoulder of his bag as the other agents scrambled beside him. Everyone activated either the night vision in the visors of their helmets or the lights in their packs. "We'll take the front of this freighter," he explained and nodded to the door that led below deck. "Stick together for now and remember this is not a research or recon mission. If you see a terror, obliterate it." Each team member nodded their understanding and followed in silence as he led them into the vessel.

CHAPTER NINE

Johnny looked at the purple woman with apprehension and curiosity. "Are you friend or foe?" he asked.

"What are you? Military all of a sudden?" Vic snarked.

"My name is Catherine. I'm a voodoo priestess and friend of Big Daddy and your other friends," she responded. Her form looked like a purple silhouette of a human with a top hat. "I'm communicating to you with help from the loa Baron Samedi."

"Do you have the baron with you?" the ghost demanded. "Where the hell is he? Where the hell are you?"

"We are in the same location, along with your friends Valerie and Aiyana," she explained. "The baron has been trapped in the domain of another keeper. He was able to seek refuge here but cannot access his realm. He believes his brother Kriminel is responsible."

The revenant sighed. "Well, I guess that's more of a confirmation than those faceless jackasses."

"Pardon?"

"We just fought some shadows," Vic explained. "Since

you're talking to us through Samedi, I guess he knows we're in his realm right now?"

Catherine nodded. "He told me he sent you there when you tried to reach out to him and he hoped you would be able to deduce what you needed to do. And he told me to tell you that you are supposed to be detectives after all."

"I see he still has his sense of humor," Johnny muttered. "What does he need us to do exactly? Finish Kriminel off for him?"

She was silent for a moment, probably hearing a voice they could not. "He says that would be nice but he does not believe you are capable of doing so."

"I hope for the sake of all souls he is a better keeper than a cheerleader." The young detective sighed and pinched the bridge of his nose.

"He says you need to free the totem to allow him to return to his realm." She began to falter and clutched her head.

"Totem? What totem?" Vic asked as she struggled. "Are you all right? What's wrong?"

"I'm sorry. I'm not used to doing something like this," the priestess admitted and tried to stand tall. "It is quite a strain. What were you asking?"

"You said something about a totem?" the revenant responded. "Is this something Kriminel made or is it a super-special artifact or something?"

"It is Samedi's tether—his key to his realm. If it is destroyed, it would destroy him." She seemed to find it difficult to keep her eyes open.

"Whoa—what? If Kriminel has it, why hasn't he already destroyed it?" the ghost asked.

"He does not have the means to do so without his power. Samedi says he is not even sure how he was able to cross into his realm with his crux destroyed. But Kriminel is crafty, and just because he has not destroyed the totem yet does not mean he won't find a way to do so. He has already managed to cut Samedi off from it—ah!" She yelped and her form sagged.

The partners knelt quickly beside her. "Hey, don't wear yourself out now," Johnny cautioned.

She nodded slowly. "I'm sorry. I must go. I cannot manage the strain much longer." She took Johnny's hand and looked at him. "Valerie and Aiyana both wish you well and promise to deal with things in New Orleans, along with Marco."

"Thank you," he said and squeezed her hand. "Tell them we'll get this done and meet them soon. This is all almost over."

Catherine nodded and smiled "They believe you." She began to fade. "The totem! It is in the shape of a mask and is most likely in Samedi's abode toward the center of the temple. Free it and he can come to your aid and we can be done with Kriminel."

"That sounds fantastic," Vic replied. "We don't need any more inspiration than that. We're on it." She nodded and faded quickly from their view. They looked toward the horizon and were able to see something gold far off in the distance. "We should probably have asked for directions." He pointed to the object. "But do you wanna make a bet that's at least something of interest?"

Johnny drew his gun. "It's better than simply standing here and at least we have a plan now."

"If we're looking for this totem of Samedi's, I doubt Kriminel will simply leave it lying around unguarded," his partner warned. "We'll probably still have to face him."

The revenant shrugged and began to march forward. "That's fine by me. It means I'll get a good look at his face before Samedi smashes it in."

Catherine pulled the hat off and tossed it away before she fell back. Valerie and Aiyana were there to catch her. "My apologies, Baron," she said weakly and leaned forward. "I could not hold on much longer."

Samedi shook his head and picked his hat up. "There is no need to worry, child. You did very well. It was a lot to ask." He placed his hat on and sighed. "It must be a sad sight, eh? Seeing a mighty loa forced to find workarounds and request the aid of his worshipers. It's not the grand sight you expected, hmm?"

She responded with a small smile. "I can't say I expected any of this. I knew you and Kriminel had your differences but this is...something beyond tragic." She shifted to her knees and bowed. "But do not trouble yourself, Baron Samedi. You have fought this with all you have, I know it. Once that demon is gone, you will be yourself again. And even if you are not, you have helped me so much already, this is the least I can do."

The look on the baron's face bordered on awestruck. He coughed and straightened his suit. "I will...eh, thank you, child." He bowed solemnly. "I still have much to do to truly fix what has been broken, even after dealing with my brother. But it is certainly nice to be appreciated for the moment. That Johnny boy and his friend Vic are a little dry for my tastes." He stood and extended a hand to help Catherine to her feet. "You should all go now. You are needed in New Orleans."

"You are right." Aiyana nodded.

Valerie held a hand up. "Before we leave, can you give us any clues to the Axman's location?" she asked. "He took Annie and disappeared. I have reports that people saw an odd light traveling out of the city but I don't know where it could have gone to."

"An odd light? And out of the city?" Samedi stroked his chin. "The Axman had a few hideouts. I was never able to identify them because of Kriminel's interference, but I doubt he had many outside his hunting grounds. I also doubt he would remain in the city with everyone looking for him."

He clicked his tongue a few times in thought before he snapped his fingers. "This could be something. Since I've kept an eye on Johnny and Vic all this time, I've seen their travels during this investigation. A couple of days ago, they encountered a witch in the forest."

"That's right—the one with the scarecrows," Aiyana exclaimed.

Samedi clapped. "Ah, yes indeed. You were there."

The shaman nodded. "I was but as I recall, the Axman wanted nothing to do with her."

"That is true, but it is free real estate, no?" The loa nodded. "And she was knowledgeable about sigils and runes and all that. The Axman has used them extensively, so such a space would appeal to him."

Valerie nodded. "I remember Donovan telling me the theater they found was full of runes and books on it. Maybe the Axman is looking for a way to gain power without Kriminel."

He snorted and folded his arms. "They were both simply using each other. They might have had a united goal but they had different ways in which they wanted to accomplish it. It would not surprise me if the Axman has indeed found a way around his need for my brother's powers."

"The question is whether we can stop him before he can do whatever that is," the shaman stated bluntly.

"We need to head back." Valerie looked at Catherine. "Are you okay?"

The priestess nodded. "I'm all right." She looked at the loa. "Will you be okay here, Baron Samedi?"

He chuckled and looked at the purple grass. "This isn't my personal choice in scenery but I'll be fine, child. As much as I like sounding off about those two detectives, I do believe in them. They've let me down, of course, but they bounce back well." He removed his hat and bowed to the women. "Go on now and do what you need to do. I will uphold my end of the bargain and finish Kriminel and join you to put an end to the Axman." He raised his head and put his hat on. "No deals necessary."

Valerie nodded to him as the three took one another's hands. "We'll hold you to that," she vowed as they disappeared.

Samedi snorted and folded his arms. "She's a saucy one, that officer. People don't respect keepers like they used to," he bemoaned although a smile lingered on his face.

"Checking room," Anderson stated over comms as the unlatching of a door could be heard. "Clear."

"So far, nothing," Falco muttered as he opened the next door. "Checking…clear."

"Do you think they all simply left?" Coleman asked. "Maybe to find another haunt?"

Donovan marked an X on a room with a highlighter. "It's possible. The drowned can be nomadic but they don't exactly move all that quickly. Rick received the message when we finished at the theater. I would say it is likely they are still around."

"Maybe we got lucky with this side of the ship," another agent suggested. "All rooms in this section are clear."

The lead agent frowned and tapped the commlink in his ear to activate it. "Rick, you guys have already boarded, right?"

There was a crackle for a moment before a dry voice replied, "Yeah, about fifteen minutes ago and have found bubkis. Would you guys settle down?"

"Is something wrong over there?"

"Nah, it's only some of the guys getting itchy trigger fingers and we haven't heard a damn— Wait a minute. Do you hear this?"

Donovan listened for a moment but heard nothing but the crackle of the comms. "Hear what?"

"That howling or moaning or whatever. Let me see if I can get it on the speaker." The agent listened closely and finally heard a faint, drawn-out moan in the comms. "Did you get it that time?"

"I did and it's definitely the sound of a drowned," he confirmed.

"Terrific," Rick replied sarcastically.

"Where is it coming from? Above, below, or on your level?"

"It sounds like below—way below," the mafioso told him. "We hear it through vents and pipes and whatnot. Hey! I got ten grand for anyone who wants to ghost up and go looking for whatever is making that racket."

"Don't do that!" Donovan snapped. "I thought I told you ghosts are as liable to get absorbed by drowned as humans are."

"Yeah, but thought it couldn't hurt me and we'd get some idea of the location. It doesn't matter anyway. I don't have any takers in this group of wimps." He sighed. "All right, what do you wanna do? Have you found anything on your side?"

"Negative, and we're almost at the front." He looked at his team. "We still have to sweep through the other side but if we have something, I think we should go together before we get too much distance between us."

He heard what sounded like the flicking of a lighter on the other end of the comms. "Christ, are they that bad?"

"Yeah." He nodded, even though the mobster wouldn't see him. "They aren't particularly fast or smart but you saw that video. If they get their stretchy hands on you, then you are as good as done. They can also take a hell of a beating so you always want to shoot at them from a safe distance."

Rick took a puff of something. "If we didn't have valuable cargo on this ship, I'd recommend simply blowing it to hell."

"Even with the cargo, I would recommend it if it did any good," Donovan admitted. "It might deal with the drowned assuming you have enough spectral explosives. But we don't know if they are the only hostiles on board."

"We've discussed that," the mobster told him. "I showed the video to some of my guys. We have a real book-smart type named Jake who had some suspicions as to what the ashes thing could be. Hey, Jake. Come over here and tell the agents what you thought. Hey, Jake! Where is that squirmy little— Wait a minute...where is Sam?"

"Rick? What's going on?" the agent demanded and gestured to his team. "Are your men missing?"

"Did they take a smoke break? We're on the clock, people. Christ! We need to get to—what's this shit on the floor?"

Another voice yelled loudly, "Boss, above you!"

"What? Oh, fuck!" Gunshots exploded over the comms and were followed shortly by nothing but static.

"Rick? Dammit. Get to the other side of the ship now!" Donovan ordered as he and the other agents raced to the other side of the vessel.

CHAPTER TEN

The mafia suddenly faced three drowned that had dropped from cracks in the ceiling. They were ugly—uglier than almost anything Rick had seen before, and he had seen burned zombie flesh a few hours earlier.

They all slouched and two of them seemed to have one arm bigger than the other. The third had two long arms that dragged along the floor and left some kind of gunk in its wake. Their light-blue bodies were bloated and blue or white phantasma flashed through them, and their faces were sunken with no eyes or lights in the sockets and nothing but a gaping void for a mouth.

His men were visible inside two of them. Sam and Jake tried to fight to free themselves. They attempted to fire their weapons but with no effect like the guns were jammed. That didn't happen with ghost weapons.

One of his men ran up. "Boss, I got a bomb. Should I throw it?"

Rick snapped his head around to look at him. "Are you a moron? That'll take us with it in this small space."

"But what about Sammy and Jake?"

"Even if it did kill these freaks it would probably take them too." He hissed in frustration but paused when he noticed a stick in the back pocket of one of his soldiers. When he realized what it was, he looked speculatively at the drowned. They at least appeared to be made of water so it was certainly worth a try.

He hurried forward and took the baton out of the mobster's pocket, pressed a switch to extend it, and squeezed the trigger. It sparked with ecto electricity. He pushed between his men and yelled for them to get the hell out of the way as he ran toward the drowned.

The one with the long arms raised one and it elongated toward him. Rick ghosted through the wall beside him and floated quickly through the narrow gap between the walls until he emerged behind them. He became tangible again and thrust the baton into the back of the head of one of the beings. It seized, began to shake, and made blubbering noises the longer he held the button down. Finally, its engorged stomach burst open and Jake fell out.

"Hell, yeah! Take that, you scummy—shit!" His other arm had been snagged by the long-armed drowned, whose head had turned completely to stare at him as it retracted its arm and pulled him toward it. He tried to fire his gun although it was trapped in its arm but like Jake and Sam's, it wouldn't go off.

"Boss!" one of the gang members shouted as another pulled Jake to safety.

He raised the baton to activate it but realized it didn't have much power left. He threw it to the man who'd called out. "Get Sam! I still got time."

Rick slid his free hand into his jacket and retrieved his pistol loaded with ether rounds. He aimed and prepared to shoot the terror in its rotting, seaweed-encrusted face when something snatched his hand and pulled him in the opposite direction.

The drowned he thought he'd blown up was still moving and worse, was reforming, although it was currently only the upper half of its body. He was now being pulled between the two and felt like he would be ripped apart.

"I get it. You both want a piece of me. Make a line and I'll beat your asses in due time." He cursed as he tried to fight against their pulls.

"Doesn't anyone else have a baton?" one of the mobsters demanded. They fired a concerted barrage at their attackers but the terrors seemed to absorb the spectral rounds when they sank into their bodies. Rick heard a pop and saw Sam being carried out by two of his comrades.

"To hell with it. Use the bombs," he ordered and continued to struggle as the drowned on the floor seemed to finally give up trying to take him and allowed the long-armed one to reel him in.

"But boss, what about you?"

"I don't give a damn!" he yelled and kicked a foot into the being's stomach but only succeeded in getting himself further entrapped. "I ain't going to be these freaks' TV dinner. Blow them to hell with me!"

Without warning, the drowned was blown apart. Rick sprawled on the floor in shock and covered in spectral water. Almost immediately, he was pulled in the opposite direction by the other creature. He retrieved his machine gun, aimed at his captor's face, and pulled the trigger to damn near empty it into the half-destroyed drowned. Its head jerked from the impact of the rounds and its hold weakened enough for him to pull his other arm and pistol out of its grasp. He fired two ether shots into its face and it seemed to melt and become nothing more than a puddle.

Rick flipped and scowled when he noticed that the terror that had swallowed Sammy was reforming. He aimed and was about to fire when something that resembled a laser blast struck it and it exploded to spew more spectral water on him. A pair of boots approached him as he coughed and hacked. Donovan bent down and offered him a hand. "Nice work. Disgusting bitches, aren't they?"

He looked at the hand for a moment before he sighed and took it. "You're not covered in their flop sweat," he muttered as the man pulled him up.

The agent looked at Jake and Sam and noticed how wet they were. "I see a couple of your men were taken. How did you get them out?"

Rick wiped some of the water off his skeletal face. "We used a baton charged with ecto electricity. I realized they are water, right? Water conducts electricity and all that? I wasn't much for schoolin' but decided giving it a shot was better than letting my boys be turned into their next meal."

Donovan nodded. "Nice work and good thinking. Ecto electricity is the way to go, along with ecto bullets. Spectral rounds can work but it looks like these guys were well fed, which means they are even tougher than normal drowned. I probably should have explained that before we boarded."

The mobster shrugged. "It could have been helpful, yeah. But we were all itching to get this done, I guess," he admitted, removed his hat, and waved it from side to side in an attempt to dry it. "Thanks for getting here when you did. I was down to simply taking the bastards with me."

"I heard that," the agent admitted. "Respect, and it was probably a good decision. I've seen what they can do and no pun intended, it's a haunting sight."

Rick checked his guns. He holstered his pistol and reloaded his machine gun with a silver magazine. "I wish we had more of those batons or something."

"Didn't you have that in your stash?"

He pulled the slide on his gun back and checked the sights. "Nuh-uh. We got spectral explosives, a good supply of ether rounds, some machine guns and shotguns, more explosives—but these have stygia—along with some stygia blades and physical ammo in case there were zombies or something. I think the baton was Antonio's walking around stick. It wasn't even fully charged."

Donovan nodded and retrieved a baton from his belt. "This can deliver ecto electricity, along with a few other options." He spun it and handed it to Rick. "Just in case. Although it isn't spectral so if you go ghost, it'll fall off."

"Yeah, I know how to be a ghost, buddy." The mobster studied it for a moment before he took it, extended it, and swung it a few times. He nodded appreciatively. "You agents sure get some fancy toys, don't you?"

"That's standard-issue," the man revealed with a smirk before he thumbed at his team. "We'll take a look downstairs."

"You don't think that was the load of them?" Rick asked and betrayed a little fatigue in his question.

Donovan shook his head and shouldered his rifle.

"Sorry, but no. We haven't seen a single member of the crew yet—alive, dead, or undead. Three drowned won't clear a freighter in a matter of hours. If it was only the three of them, your onboard guards could probably have dealt with them if they had ether rounds, which I assume is fairly standard in the mafia."

Rick shortened the baton and shrugged dismissively as he clipped it to his belt. "About as standard as it is for the cops."

"Well, that's a good thing in this case because there are most certainly more of them." As if on cue, a low moan echoed eerily from deeper in the ship. He checked his rifle. "I understand if you need a breather after all that."

The mobster cocked his head. "Taking a breather isn't an option for a ghost, no pun intended. Sam and Jake may need a chance to take it easy—"

"I will rip the heart out of the next one of those watery bitches I see!" Sammy roared and a couple of his comrades attempted to calm him.

"Or not." Rick chuckled. "But I'm still good." He aimed his gun at the ceiling. "And I want a little more revenge. You shot the one that was fixing to eat me, after all."

Donovan grinned and nodded in understanding. "I get you. I think it is better if we stick together from now on. It might take a little longer, but since we don't have full knowledge of what is waiting for us down below, it's probably for the best."

"Fair enough." The ghost mobster nodded and his gaze darted away. "I talked to the ghost captain, Sully. He says that as long as nothing is too busted on the ship, he can probably bring it to port if we clear everything out."

"Okay, that sounds good. We have a plan so shall we get started?"

Donovan turned to walk away but Rick blurted quickly "We didn't screw with the Agency!"

The agent stopped. "Do what?"

Rick leaned against the wall and folded his arms. "I know the rumors swirling around. The Agency is looking at us—the ghost mafia and specifically the New Orleans branch—as the ones who screwed with your databases and files and whatnot, right? I can tell you it wasn't us."

"Is that right?" The man turned to look at him. "I'm not trying to mock you or anything, but I didn't think you were high up enough to know anything like that."

"Technically, I wasn't until this whole mess started. I was a part of one of the old head's inner circle." He rolled his lights. "We've gone through four heads of the NO mob in three months—ain't that something? Anyway, I do know that we considered calling you in ourselves at one point, but with leadership changes and all that, it never happened. Plus, protection is one of our services and if we can't provide that when we need to, it's kind of hard to make good deals."

He sighed and tilted his hat down. "I don't know why, but I wanted to make sure you didn't think we would stab you guys in the back once all this is done. I know this is only a temporary truce and you, us, and the cops will go back to our little triangle of fucking with one another after this is over, but... Well, don't think we aren't capable of being civil, all right?"

Donovan was honestly quite stunned for a moment, but

he responded with a friendly grin. "I assume you don't want me to tell anybody you told me this?"

"If you don't mind. I still have a rep to protect."

The agent shrugged. "I'm not sure I can convince anyone in high command about the truth of it without a testimony but I'll certainly keep it in mind." He began to walk to his team before he stopped for a moment and said, "By the way, the civil thing is nice and all. But seeing your loyalty? That will stick with me more."

With that, he continued and Rick looked away. "Damn, sticking your neck out for your boys is a big show of loyalty to him? I know people think the mob is a shady group, but if you can't count on your people to help you out in a jam, what good is a group like that?"

CHAPTER ELEVEN

Annie lay on a rotting table, groggy and out of sorts, and something—maybe water?—dripped on her. She had no idea where she was and didn't remember walking there or being brought. When she tried to rise, she seemed to be stuck to the table and it took a few moments for her to realize that some kind of dark energy bound her there.

"You are awake, I see." The coarse voice had rapidly become familiar. She turned her head to look at the Axman and her eyes widened. He now looked how she remembered him—tall and coursing with his black phantasma.

"Your powers...you got them back?" she asked and strained against the bonds. "What's going on?"

He tilted his head. "You're beautiful but not very bright, are you, my dear?" He held a hand up. "I'm finishing my plan. Together, we will bring down the barrier between life and death and make both concepts antiquated. We will make the afterlife and places like Hell and Heaven nothing more than fantasy from here on." He walked to her side and light formed around his fingers.

"You did all this simply to escape Hell and the fate you earned by killing innocent people?" She tried to stall him in hopes that someone would come in at the last moment.

When he leaned toward her, the lights in his eyes consumed her vision. "If it helps, not all were innocent like you." He raised his arm. "And that is what I need from you." His arm swung down, pierced her chest, and left no breath for her to scream.

She awoke with a start and drew deep, ragged breaths as she looked around quickly. It took a long moment for her to realize she was still in the basement next to the furnace. The heavy rural smell still lingered in the air. She sighed and leaned back against the wall. It took a nightmare to make her realize she wasn't in the worst position she could be, but it was only a half-step.

He had said she was his key but she still wasn't exactly clear what that meant or at least how she was supposed to open the "lock" he needed her for. She despised it all—being in his grasp, not knowing what he wanted with her, and the fact that she was putting her brother and new friends in harm's way. They would come for her, she knew this, and while that should have brought some comfort, she was also fairly sure the Axman knew it too. He might be arrogant but he wouldn't have come this far if he was foolish.

Annie had picked at the ropes, but it had not accomplished much other than rub the tips of some of her fingers raw. Despite the disrepair of the room she was in there was nothing nearby that was broken or jagged that she could use to cut through them, and she didn't have the strength to knock the furnace apart. She was stuck in a limbo of her own, waiting to see who would get to her first.

A part of her wanted it done either way. This last week had been one of escalating chaos, and to see the pain it caused everyone merely made it worse. But she would not succumb to that. If the Axman won, that pain would not stop. It would only grow along with a cavalcade of other horrors. She would believe in her friends, that she would get out of this, and that she would have her chance to smash that boney bastard in the face for her troubles.

Although now that she had been on her own for some time with only a jug of water and some bowls of cheese and soup for company, she grew anxious. Where had he gone and what was he doing?

"No! Wait—please!" the man cried but the Axman swung his namesake weapon into his skull. He held his victim's neck firm while black phantasma enveloped it and drained his soul from him. When he tossed the corpse to the side, he looked at the other four bodies—all junkies he happened to stumble across—and felt sickened. Only a day earlier, he could kill anyone he needed to and get the highest quality souls, those who had led rich lives or were powerful through their hard work and the power that came with it.

Now, he was forced into taking the dregs to get his souls and felt like he was feasting on rats in an alley simply to sate his hunger. He walked to one of the boarded windows and peered through the cracks at the void in the sky. They were so close and the damned loa had to screw everything up. He hadn't heard from him at all so perhaps he had been slain by his brother or the Wild Hunt. That triggered a fairly audacious thought and he paused to consider the possibility that he might have another option.

Kriminel had gone to deal with the Wild Hunt and there was a good chance some had fallen through the portal. They would be very, very strong souls for him to take—assuming he could prevail against them in his current condition. He would have to catch one or maybe two by surprise, but they would provide him with the energy he needed to finish his first objective and restore his previous form.

There was considerable risk with this plan since he was forced to stick to the shadows as he essentially had the whole city and four different factions out looking for him. Not only that, but his tussle with the mafia would have them all on even higher alert now that they were working together. He doubted that the Hunt was a part of the alliance, however.

It certainly was worth exploring. He turned, kicked a couple of the corpses out of the way, and took some chalk from his pants pocket. Focused now, he drew a sigil on the floor, placed his palm on it, and let a little of his phantasma cover it. A group of shades came through and flew quickly out of the drug den.

He had a way to find them. The Wild Hunt's entire mission was to take care of terrors both in Limbo and the living world, and hordes of them were loose in the city now. His mood began to brighten when he considered how many entities of all types would unwittingly aid him.

His quarry would be scattered to be able to deal with them and all he needed was one. He found a dusty couch and sat while he explored his bond to the shades and saw what they did as they flew through the city. Sooner or later, they would find one and he was willing to wait a little longer.

Luckily for him, it appeared that fortune still gave him a half-smile as one of the shades came across a figure in ancient armor and a horned helmet. He was either a member of the Wild Hunt or a rather dramatic ghost hunter. With a deftness that spoke of skill and experience, he sliced through what appeared to be a banshee and it fell apart and vanished. He turned his attention to the shade, took a spear from a bundle on his back, and launched it. In an instant, the bond was severed.

The Axman pushed to his feet, checked his equipment, and took stock of the energy he had left. He was certainly not a fighter but he was a killer. If there was one thing having almost unrivaled power had taught him, it was understanding that sometimes, it was better to kill or maim before the fight even started. It turned an enemy into a victim much faster. He would get the soul he needed this time and he would get his new life soon after.

"What are you packing?" Vic asked as they drew closer to the large building. "Anything special?"

Johnny shook his head. "It's not like we had the time to

stock up before we came here. I still have the ecto fire cartridge but beyond that, merely the normal ether ones. You?"

The ghost detective checked the box on his belt that held his special bullets. "Ecto fire, shock, and freeze—a couple of each. A few more ether rounds. It's not much but we are dealing with a depowered loa."

"So that means he isn't much of a threat?"

His partner looked at him and his eyes dimmed. "I wouldn't go that far. He might not be as powerful as he was but he's still crafty and capable of more things than a normal ghost like me. The plan is still to focus on the totem and get Samedi in here to put his brother in timeout."

They pushed through large leaves and stopped to stare at a golden temple adorned with skulls and surrounded by various styles of tombstones. There were some drawings, mostly of Samedi but also what appeared to be other loas, including one with several scratches along the face to disfigure it. The ghost frowned. "Do you think this is the place?"

"I'd be willing to bet money," Johnny confirmed as he studied a rather ornate diamond-encrusted skull near the entrance. "But I don't see any shadows. I doubt he doesn't know we're here."

Vic held a finger to his mouth and motioned quickly for him to follow. They darted around the side of the entrance behind a statue of a female loa and he pointed to something in the distance. The young detective wanted to shake his head. Of course, he had to jinx it. Several shadows floated around the corner, some wielding weapons like spiked clubs and machetes. A couple wandered past as a few split off and headed into the jungle. "It looks like we got lucky in a way," the ghost commented. "He thinks we might still be in the forest."

"He must have limited phantasma at this point, right?" the revenant stated thoughtfully. "If he's focused on creating those shadows to guard him, maybe he won't be able to fight effectively."

His partner looked at him with a questioning glance. "Are you coming around to the idea of taking him on ourselves?"

"I'm merely preparing for the worst," he admitted and drew his gun. "I'm not entirely sure what we have to do to free this totem in the first place. If we are able to get hold of it but can't figure out what to do...well, we might have to."

Vic nodded. "Don't you hate it when the smart thing is often the pessimistic thing as well?" He looked around to make sure the coast was clear. "We'll have a better idea of what we need to do when we get eyes on it. Come on."

They darted up the stairs but hesitated when they reached the large doors that would probably make a hell of a noise if they tried to force them open. Fortunately, there were large windows close to the entrance with nothing in the way. The ghost simply floated through one of them but Johnny had to leap off the side of the wall and catch the edge. He almost slipped off but his companion caught his hand and dragged him in.

The inside of the temple looked as if it was made of glowing stone. Cracks in the floor were illuminated in either golden or purple light, which helped somewhat because the rest of the large hall was dark and they didn't even have a torch or flashlight to help. "How can we see in here?" Johnny asked.

"Huh? Is something wrong with your eyes?" Vic whispered. "It seems bright enough to me."

The revenant double-checked to make sure his eyepatch was still off. "It must be a ghost thing. I can see the glow on the ground but everything else is dark."

"It's probably more like a living thing since this is the domain of a keeper," his partner pointed out and began to walk down the hall. "Come on. I'll lead you through." They proceeded cautiously and took routes that lead them deeper into the temple and as close to the center as possible.

Along the way, they occasionally encountered a shadow, but Johnny began to notice something odd about them. "Is it only me or do they look...drunk?" he asked as one hobbled past them with a slow, weary step.

"I wonder if that has something to do with them or Kriminel," Vic responded. "Maybe that could be our plan— get Kriminel good and sloshed and we wouldn't have to worry about him."

"How much liquor would it take to get a former keeper blackout drunk?"

The ghost detective checked his pockets. "Certainly more than I would have in my flask if I hadn't left it on the other side." He shuddered and raised his head sharply to look down the left hall. "What the hell was that?"

"What?" Johnny looked down the hall and saw only more darkness, but his partner turned into it quickly and left him to follow. This corridor seemed to stretch farther than the others and at first, he continued to not feel or see what had caught his companion's attention. He did, however, feel a growing sense of unease as they proceeded deeper into the temple. It wasn't helped by the rather violent images he saw on the walls in the low lighting. "Vic, where the hell are we going?"

His partner held a finger up and pointed forward. "You can't see that?" he asked.

The revenant squinted but it still all looked like darkness to him. After a moment, he could see something swirling in it. As they got closer, he could see a dim violet light in the darkness but it was also evident that it wasn't merely cloaked by the shadows.

"I guess we now know why Samedi has a hard time coming over," the ghost muttered.

They stepped into the chamber, a round room with a pit in the middle. Above this, the totem hovered, a smiling mask with white, black, and purple lines similar to the baron's face paint and attached to a golden staff. It was surrounded by some kind of tornado of dark energy that whipped furiously around it but oddly made no sound, at least that Johnny could hear.

"What is that?"

"Kriminel's handiwork," Vic replied and cocked his head as he pulled his jacket closed. "That's about all I can tell you."

The young detective looked at his partner, who was shivering. "Are you cold?"

"Yeah, of course I am. Don't you feel—wait, I'm cold?" His lights widened. "That ain't normal."

"No kidding." Johnny caught a gleam beneath him and

looked at a spiral-like design etched into the floor that glowed red. "It's a sigil."

Vic frowned. "Red is Kriminel's color." He looked at the vortex. "It's probably what he's using to keep this going."

He took his gun out and the ecto fire cartridge and looked at the ghost. "Do you think if we burn it off we can shut it down and free the totem?"

His partner shrugged. "It's better than what I was thinking."

"Which was?"

"I would float up to it and try to reach through."

Johnny motioned for him to step back. "Yeah, let's go with my idea first." He aimed at the sigil and fired, and a torrent of green flame flowed out of the weapon. It engulfed the sigil but as he began to smile, his glee disappeared when he saw it absorbed into the sigil and a new emblem appeared around it.

"Get out of the way, kid," Vic warned, dove forward, and knocked them both to the floor as all the fire—colored red now—spat out, struck the roof, and disappeared.

"What was that?" the young detective asked as he looked at his gun and then the sigil.

His partner stood and helped him up. "It's a safety measure of some kind. I'm not exactly an expert when it comes to sigils and the mystical stuff but I've seen that. It blows things back like a reflector. Normally, ecto fire wouldn't hurt a living person but it looks like Kriminel did something to it."

He looked at the ceiling that still blazed a fiery red color. "Do you think he was expecting us or simply being paranoid?"

"I'm sure he knows his brother won't let him crash here uncontested," Vic replied and they both heard a series of agitated moans from around them. They held their guns up as dark figures came down the halls. It seems the shadows had been alerted to their presence. They prepared to fire when large doors across the chamber flew open and a familiar figure stormed in. His skin was ragged and his red-and-black face paint was smeared. It looked like he had lost several feet in height but he was still at least a foot taller than either of the partners.

"Well now," Kriminel growled as two shadows floated over him. "If it isn't my brother's little pets."

CHAPTER TWELVE

Valerie, Marco, and Aiyana stepped out of the patrol car and all stared at the woods awaiting them. "Are you sure this is the place, Aiyana?" the officer asked as she shut the door.

"Positive," she replied and retrieved a white totem. "The witch's abode should not be far but we need to be wary. Even if the Axman is not here, there could be any number of traps the witch made before she died that are still active."

Marco shouldered his bat. "Walking rotters waiting for us, right?" He scowled and craned his neck. "It's not that big a deal. I don't care if there are demons in the way. I will get to my sister."

"Don't worry, Marco," Valerie assured him, popped the trunk, and took out the shotgun she had procured from the armory. "If she's here, we won't leave without her."

"Agreed," Aiyana replied as a glowing orb floated out of the totem. "But we need to be on guard. We won't be of any help if we can't get to her at all." The orb floated a few yards ahead of them and Aiyana followed it, the other two walking closely behind her.

"You and Johnny already came through here, right?" Marco asked as they moved into the woods. "Is there anything to worry about? You took care of it last time."

The shaman glanced at him. "You are forgetting that the Axman is potentially here now. If the witch left anything I'm sure he would make use of it." She looked into the sky. "On top of the terrors now roaming free, we have much to look out for."

Valerie looked at the orb. "So what's with the Christmas light?"

"It is a guide," she explained, a hint of laughter in her voice at the comparison. "To look for any potential illusions that may be cast and to warn us of supernatural dangers."

"So magic is a thing, huh?" Marco commented. "I can't get my head wrapped around that."

The officer chuckled. "You can set your bat on fire and you have a hard time believing in magic?"

"That's only a party trick," he replied. "Besides, most people in my family can do it, at least since the veil weakened back in the day. And it's only an empath. It is one thing that works on ghosts. I can't do a bunch of stuff like Aiyana or a witch can."

"To be fair, my abilities work in a similar fashion to an empath," the shaman explained as she stepped over a dead branch. "And it is not my power at all. I channel the powers of the spirits."

He considered this and grinned. "Is that right? Next

time we run into the Axman, see if any one of them care to chokeslam the bastard back to hell."

"If they could do so, I'm sure they would be happy to oblige." Aiyana came to a stop and narrowed her eyes as the orb floated around a tree. She held a hand up and it was engulfed in white flames before she approached cautiously and stared at the trunk. After a moment, she beckoned to the other two.

"What is it?" Valerie asked as they approached.

"A sigil." The three looked at two intercrossed triangles inside a square with jagged ends. "I believe it is some kind of ward—a shield."

"A shield?" Marco asked and looked confused. "Against what?"

"If it was made by the witch, could it have been to protect herself against the Axman?" the officer asked.

Aiyana shook her head quickly. "I do not believe so. She was enthralled by him although he seemed to have no interest in her." She held her flaming hand up to it but backed it away slowly. "Witches, like all spirit callers, are neither inherently evil or good. But for one such as her who seemed to forcefully control spirits rather than work with them, she would make some enemies."

"Other spirit callers?" Valerie asked.

The shaman shook her head. "We do look out for one another and if we know of another caller misusing their powers and breaking bonds, we are known to take care of them for the sake of balance. But a sigil like this would have no control or negative effect on us. This was protection against some type of terror."

Marco tapped the sigil with his bat. "Well, that's a good

thing then, right? With all the terrors running around, we don't have to worry about running into them with this up, now do we?"

"Not necessarily." Aiyana shrugged and continued to move forward. "Given that it is not active."

"Do what?" he asked as he trailed behind the other two. "Then why did your little light ball stop at it?"

"There was some residual phantasma left but it is not enough to keep it going," she explained but her hand was still alight. "We may get lucky. With the witch gone, whatever she was trying to hide from may have no reason to be here."

Valerie frowned and looked at the crack in the sky. "I wouldn't say we've been very lucky recently."

The shaman looked deeper into the forest and squinted at something just out of her vision. She wondered if something was truly there or if it was simply her paranoia growing. "I would have to agree with you."

"How much farther, Sam?" Rick asked as the group of agents and mobsters descended into the deeper areas of the freighter. Their trek had been less intense since they banded together. They had fought only two more drowned along the way and they were both alone, which made it almost child's play as the watery terrors were lost under a barrage of lasers and spectral shots.

But now they were more than a little concerned. Donovan was sure that a freighter with a crew—even if it was half a crew—could not have been overcome by only a handful of drowned. He also wanted to ask Jake about his idea of what the "ashes" monster could be but the mobster still seemed out of it. While he refused to return to Bobby's ship, he had kept to himself since the attack.

"We still got the other half of the boat, Rick," Sam pointed out, peeked into an empty supply room, and closed the door. "But I guess you're asking about the heat?"

Rick nodded. "We still have a good amount. But with those weapons, we can do some real damage when we find the rest of those muddy dicks."

One of the mobsters turned his head with a quizzical expression. "Muddy dicks?"

The ghost waved a hand in irritation. "Ah, give me a break. I'm not at the top of my game right now."

"You have gone through a rolodex of insults," Donovan commented. "Speaking of the heat, what kind of weapons were you guys bringing in exactly?"

"Very good ones," the mob leader replied and shrugged when he looked at him. "Look, I wasn't in charge of this. Hell, I wasn't even the muscle until they ran out of guys. Yesterday, I was only supposed to show up and get everything situated. Now, I gotta retrieve the damn things. All I know is this order went through when the Axman attacks were beginning so whatever they are, they were bought here to deal with that son of a bitch."

"I would think the only thing that could do that would be Agency weapons," Coleman interjected.

"Or they could be mementos," one of the mobsters added. A few of the group looked at him and he lowered his hat a little self-consciously. "Well...uh, I mean they can be powerful if they have the right memories attached to them and all. The Axman is using one too, right?"

The agent nodded. "Yeah, he is. You're Jake, right?"

He didn't respond but Rick nodded. "Yeah, that's him. He's a good kid and one of the resident nerds in our division. He has a good head for the Limbo market and looking into those terrors when we need a job done. Although he's a little on the mousey side, he's only been with us for a few years. We'll get him barrel-chested one of these days."

"He even volunteered to run with us a few months ago," Sam added and dropped back to clap him on the back. "It's a hell of a thing to experience in your first few months running with the big boys, right, kid?"

Jake nodded and pretended to check his gun. "Yeah, that's one way to put it."

"And you got the boss to save your neck."

His lights brightened. "That's right. I wanted to thank you, sir, for—"

"There's no need, kid," Rick said before he could finish. "When we're done and drinks are going around, I won't mind the praise. But until then, we're still in this mess, so let's focus on keeping ourselves out of those water zombies' guts."

He nodded and pulled his hat down again. "Uh, right. I agree with you there, boss."

"If you don't mind me asking," Donovan began while he motioned to a couple of agents to check the rooms around them. "Rick said you might have had an idea of what we could be dealing with."

"The drowned?" Jake frowned and shook his head. "I never ran into them before today."

"No, the other one that could be here," he replied. "The one that turned people to ash."

His lights dimmed but widened. "Oh, right. That. I… um, I thought it over and I couldn't think of anything that did something like that."

"Same here," Donovan agreed. "I've wracked my brain but nothing comes to mind. And believe me, in the SEA, knowing the numerous varieties of terrors is standard."

Jake nodded. "I can believe it, sir. But that got me thinking. Maybe the crew didn't know what they saw."

"Didn't know what they saw?" Rick asked and snorted. "I'm sure they were scared shitless but even then, when you see someone turned into ash, there's isn't much you can confuse that with—gah!" He wasn't paying attention to where he was going and accidentally ghosted through a wall at a sharp turn, but that wasn't what startled him. He reappeared quickly and pointed at the wall. "They're in there!"

Donovan and the agents primed their weapons. "What are?"

"More of those drowned," the mobster told them. "It's dark in there but I saw dozens of the bitches—all of them with bloated stomachs."

"It explains why everything has been so quiet," Anderson commented.

The agent leader nodded. "Yeah, they've been digesting."

Sam shuddered and readied his weapon reflexively. "Sheesh, that's a bad way to go."

"It could have been us," Jake muttered and Sam nodded.

"They are all huddled in there." Rick pointed at three of the mobsters and beckoned them closer. "I say we simply blow them back to hell."

"Technically, you are obliterating them," Donovan corrected. "But it works all the same."

"And works better for me. Even if I draw the short straw and get sent there myself, I would feel a little better if I didn't see them again."

He snapped his fingers and the three mobsters shrugged their packs off and withdrew bundles of glowing blue dynamite-looking sticks that they handed to each other.

"Let's go around the side," Rick suggested. "If we go through the wall, they are right there. I almost bumped into one when I ghosted in. But if we enter through the front, we can toss them inside and get the hell out of the way before they blow. Those chumps got long limbs but they sure as hell aren't fast." He paused and looked at Donovan. "Right?"

The agent nodded. "Certainly not when they're feeding. But make sure you don't get grabbed."

The mobster shook his head, dug in his coat pocket, and took a lighter out. He flicked it a few times before a green flame appeared. "They won't get the chance. And you guys should get back for when the explosion goes off. Well, the ghosts should. You agents might only feel a tickle. Come on boys."

Donovan felt a tug on his jacket and turned to Jake. "Oh right, sorry. What were you saying?"

"I thought that maybe they weren't being turned to ash

and it only looked that way," the mobster continued and pointed at himself. "You know how ghosts turn gray if we run out of phantasma or it's drained from us? It looks like we crumble and turn to dust, right? Well, maybe this is the same idea. It's something that can drain both the phantasma from ghosts and the lifeforce from breathers to make it appear that they are turning to ashes."

"Something that drains lifeforce?" That opened the possibilities. Wraiths were a top choice but if one or a few came through the portal, they had a whole city to target. What would be something that would go all the way out to sea?

"I know they are essentially zombies and they are known for eating brains, not having them, but it is kind of weird that no one is directing them, right?" Sam asked Coleman as they walked down the hall. "All of them in there are useless until they are done...uh, feasting, I guess."

The agent nodded. "That is true and typically what happens when they group like this. I suppose the drowned we've taken care of so far could have been the guardians and came looking for us when they heard all the noise. Still, it seems like a small number to split up like that."

Jake cocked his head. "Hey, what about an undine?"

"Undine?" Donovan frowned and tried to remember the details. "I don't think I've ever run into one."

"They are a type of elemental spirit infused with corrupted phantasma or the manifestations of negative emotions of ghosts, like shades. They are looking for a soul for themselves and try to claim them from others but can't control them properly. Most times, they simply drain the life or phantasma from others."

"Like shades?" Donovan realized that what the mobster had said made sense, and they had dealt with a shit-ton of shades lately. "You could be right. We have a database of all terrors so if we run into it, we should know how to—"

"What the hell is that?" one of the mobsters shouted from the back of the group. The agents and other mafia stopped and turned back as a shriek carried through the metal hallways. Donovan's breath caught.

Gunshots rang out. "Throw the sticks!" Rick ordered and electricity sizzled in the air. "I'll knock it back but blow those drowned to hell before they get out."

The agent gestured for his team to follow him as he raced down the hall. He turned the corner and was ready to shoot on sight but froze and gaped at something he had never seen before. The figure that circled Rick and his men was long and white and appeared to be comprised of water.

At the head was a feminine form that looked much like a statue. It had a humanoid shape but all its features, including its hair, were flat and blank. Rick held it at bay with his baton while it tried repeatedly to strike. When zapped, the body moved away, but when he attempted to attack its tail, for lack of a better word, it seemed to do nothing.

The ghost mobster looked at the agent. "Donovan, wanna give us a hand?"

He snapped quickly to his senses, aimed, and fired several shots at the terror. The shots seemed somewhat effective and it recoiled from the blasts and its form became mishappen. It had blocked access to the room with the drowned but one of the mobsters was able to finally pry the door open.

He lit a bundle of explosives. "I got it, Rick!" he shouted and pulled the door ajar enough to throw the bombs in. "We gotta move. The walls ain't gonna stop the blast for us."

"I know that." The mob leader growled and lit a stick as well. "Get moving, lunks!" His men were able to float away as he raced forward and jammed the explosive into the chest of the creature. "It was nice meeting ya. Now piss off!"

He sneered as he ghosted into the floor. Donovan looked down the hall to where the other ghosts approached, but he and his team shouted for them to turn and they were able to back away as the blast went off. A wave of ether erupted all around him and even went through the ceiling and floor. The terror shuddered from the blast and seemed to lose its form before the explosive Rick had shoved into its chest detonated as well and it was blown apart and turned into a giant puddle of water.

The agent leaned against the wall to steady himself. "Is everyone all right?" he called.

"We're good, sir!" Anderson shouted in response. "The ghosts are a little rattled but they are in one piece."

"We're shaken, not rattled," Sam declared.

Donovan sighed with relief. "Good. That's something at least. And tell Jake I think he was right."

"About what?" Rick appeared from below.

The agent pointed at the puddle of white water. "I think that was the mysterious terror we were trying to find."

The mobster slid his hand into his jacket to retrieve his

cigarette case. "You don't say," he stated sarcastically, opened the case, and took one out, although he struggled to get his lighter to work. "What was it?"

"An undine or water spirit. Jake suggested it, albeit just before it appeared." Donovan explained. "I never ran into one before so I guess it was a new experience for both of us."

When he failed to light his cigarette, Rick replaced it in the box and put it away. "I'm only glad it wasn't too much trouble. Still, it's hard to believe that something like that killed the whole crew. We had guys with explosives and other weapons, both human and ghost, and they were taken out by something like that? It seems like a waste of— are you for real?"

Donovan turned and realized that the water had begun to coalesce and reform into the undine's long-tailed body. He aimed as Rick reached for his machine gun. "It looks like they might have had more trouble than we thought."

CHAPTER THIRTEEN

Viking sank his ax into the head of the ghoul before he dragged it down and tore the entity in two. He let the two halves fall as he shouldered his weapon and looked at several others in the distance. His inclination was to move and deal with them but he felt something far worse than a simple terror nearby.

"Will you simply hide?" He growled and looked over his shoulder. "Perhaps it is natural for a rat like yourself."

"Is that what you think of me?" The Axman emerged from the shadows of the alley and leaned against a damaged car. "I think I've done far more than a simple rat could. Then again, the black plague started thanks to a rat so maybe you are onto something."

Shades appeared above the hunter and circled him but he ignored them. "I have to say, I feel many things looking at you now."

"Oh? Do you care to share?"

"Anger at what you have done, amusement that you would show your face to me so freely, morbid curiosity at what led you to be the monster you are." He grasped his ax in both hands. "And relief that I can end this chaos here and now."

The Axman held his hand out and a hatchet appeared in it. "Do you honestly think I am so easily defeated? Have you not heard what I've accomplished?"

"I am well aware of what you have done," Viking declared and stepped toward the killer, focused and determined. "In both life and death, you were nothing more than a monster—and a cowardly one at that. But I'm glad you've found a spine now so I can tear it out."

His opponent regarded him with something that suggested amusement. "Did you do this when you were alive too? These pointless boasts and threats? I guess that's the whole ancient warrior thing you have going on, hmm?"

"You should not mock it, Axman." Viking growled and paced forward slowly. "Do you think me easy prey? You do not have even half the power you did when you struck fear into this city. You are no warrior and without that power, you are merely prey!" he roared and charged.

His target responded by tossing the hatchet, which the hunter deflected easily with his ax, only to find that he couldn't lower his arms again. He looked up at two shades that held his weapon and arms up while another flung itself onto his back and covered his vision.

"Is this the best you can do?" he demanded and used his enormous strength to fling the shades that restrained him away before he grasped the one on his back and hurled it after the others. "These pests are hardly more of a challenge to me than a practice dummy. They are a mere—"

"Distraction?" the Axman asked and his voice now

came from behind the hunter. An oddly muted thud accompanied an equally strange push that made Viking stagger forward. He spun, fell heavily, and frowned when his white phantasma drifted in the air.

Confused, he raised his hand to his head. "What did you..." he muttered but the question trailed into nothing when he felt an ax buried deep into the back of his skull.

The Axman stood tall above him. "You are right, Viking." He held his hand out and one of the shades presented him with another hatchet. "I am neither as powerful as I was only a few hours ago nor a warrior. But I didn't get to where I am now due to power alone. While I might not be a warrior, I am a killer." He raised the hatchet. "And I am here to kill you, not fight you."

Viking roared, launched himself off the dirt, and pounded into his adversary, who dropped the hatchet. They collided with a storefront and he lifted his ax to deliver a killing strike. His foe merely held his hand up and the ax still buried in the hunter's head began to shake before it pulled itself free and returned to the killer's grasp.

The huntsman went still before the Axman shoved him off easily. He held his hand up and dark phantasma coated it. "I admire your conviction," he stated flatly, placed his hand on his victim's head, and drained his soul while the huntsman stared at him with wide eyes that attempted to show anger as he tried fruitlessly to push his attacker away. "Rest now, warrior," he whispered and tightened his grasp as he leaned forward to watch as Viking turned gray. "Think of this as early retirement. You would have soon been out of a job anyway." His chuckle was mocking.

He released him and the warrior sagged heavily as the

lights in his eyes dimmed. The killer looked at the soul of the huntsman he'd collected and felt a sense of manic glee return to him, a familiar response that he'd had for so long and recently lost.

"Finally," he whispered as he pushed the orb into his chest and let Viking's soul disperse over him and combine with his phantasma. Soon, the dark phantasma around his hand slunk up his arm, across his shoulders, over his head to his chest, and from there to his legs and feet. He grew in response and the ax in his hand changed form to a more malevolent and larger version. His eyes glimmered and he turned to see his reflection in a car window as he solidified his form. He had returned.

"Viking!" A cry rang out. The killer looked at two huntsmen, one in Roman armor with a sword and shield and the other in a cloak and hood who wielded a bow. He glanced at Viking's body as it withered into ashes before it vanished completely.

"It was rather unkind of him to leave like that." The Axman chuckled, tilted his head at the newcomers, and considered his options. He had been able to overcome one with deception and an almost decisive strike but it would be a little harder to do so with two. Then again, he had recovered his power but it was more like turning the clock back than refueling. It would run out again without his connection to Kriminel. He hoped that idiot hadn't gotten himself killed yet, but he could always slow the timer a tad.

He merely needed more victims.

Dark clouds began to form overhead and a low, droning, jazz tone emitted from a couple of the nearby cars. He took his ax in both hands as the huntsmen prepared to strike. They might be warriors, but he was a killer.

———

"So are we lost or is this property so far off the beaten track?" Marco muttered as the three friends continued deeper into the forest. "Who the hell sets a farm up in the middle of a janky forest anyway?"

"This is Louisiana, Marco," Valerie reminded him as she stepped over a root. "Unless it's an old farmstead, land is hard to come by. Do you think it would be better near a swamp?"

"Not in these shoes." He scowled and looked over his shoulder. "Hey, hold up." He pointed. "Is that the same sigil?"

Aiyana stopped as her orb floated closer to the mark and glowed slightly brighter. "It seems to be. But I haven't sensed or seen a spiritual presence since we got here."

"That's fine by me," Valerie stated. "All the more reason to finish this search and potentially rescue Annie before any decide to appear. Is that the field?" She walked ahead a few steps and pointed.

Her companions both looked past a line of trees to where golden crops could be seen. "I cannot think of what else it could be," the shaman responded.

He hurried forward. "It's better to find out than simply guess."

"Marco! Wait up!" the officer demanded and frowned as she drew her gun. "Let's catch up to him before he does anything rash."

Aiyana dismissed her orb and tossed the totem aside as it began to crack and fall apart. "Agreed, but we seem a little late for the latter." They rushed through the trees to where Marco had stopped at the edge of the field.

"Where the hell do we go?" he asked, tense and impatient. "I can't see anything over this stuff."

Valerie deferred to the shaman, who nodded and closed her eyes. "This appears to be the place. Let me see if I can —" Her eyes snapped open. "Something is coming."

Marco looked back. "The Axman?"

"I don't think so, but something powerful nevertheless. Quickly—into the field!" They ran through the crops. Aiyana looked up and noticed that the clouds had darkened rapidly. She recalled the rain that had accompanied the appearance of an Axman copy and wondered if he'd found more servants.

The young man glanced over his shoulder and skidded to a halt. "Uh...guys, I don't think we can outrun that." He pointed with his bat and the two women stopped and looked behind them. A ball of silver-and-green phantasma rocketed closer and thudded into the dirt in front of them, and a being emerged. It was large and bulbous with beady little eyes and a maw of spiked teeth.

"Well, who do we have here?" it demanded and its loud, guttural voice carried easily through the field. "Did Edna get herself some cronies after she cast me aside?"

"Edna?" Marco snorted and lifted his bat as the blue flames engulfed it. "Who the hell is Edna?"

"You have to be doing that bitch of a witch's will!" The monster growled and pointed a fat finger at them. "Why else would you be here?"

"Forgive me for interrupting," Aiyana called and gestured for her friends to lower their weapons. "We are not servants for the witch who used to live here."

The monstrous ghost leaned closer. "Used to?"

She nodded. "Yes, she is dead now. I was there when it happened."

It wasn't clear whether this pleased or annoyed the creature. It straightened and placed its hands on its hips. "Are you serious? I've wanted to get my now cold hands on her ever since she backstabbed me and now, she's a ghost and I'm stuck on this side?" It snorted and began to shrink and change form into a skeletal ghost in a long black dress and curved hat with purple lipstick and curled eyelashes. "Honestly, my luck sucks. I can't even have a murderous family reunion properly."

"Family reunion?" Valerie still held her gun ready but kept her finger off the trigger. "Are you a witch too?"

The ghost nodded and dug in a tiny purse. "Yeah—Edna's cousin. My name's Castecka." She retrieved a thin, jade cigarette holder and an equally thin cigarette. Once she placed it in the holder, she snapped her fingers and lit it. "I was alive not three months ago before that crazy whacko killed me. You know, I let her stay with me rent-free this last year." She turned in the direction of the farm. "Not that I exactly paid much myself. I simply cast an illusion over everything. Most who came here saw it as a dead field." She regarded them curiously. "So how can you see all this?"

"Well, she's a shaman," Marco replied casually and nodded to Aiyana. "But we're all specters."

She rolled her eyes. "Ah. Right, of course. Otherwise,

we wouldn't even be talking. Sorry, I'm still getting used to this ghost thing." She took a drag from the holder and blew out a small amount of smoke. "I was used to communicating and working with ghosts, not being one. It's more of an adjustment than I thought."

"I'm sorry, but did you say your cousin killed you?" Aiyana asked.

Castecka clenched a fist. "Yeah, she did. She was never half the witch I was and only used her knowledge to be a lazy idiot. A few months ago, she suddenly began to obsess over this creep who appeared in town, some psychopath—"

"With an ax?" Valerie interrupted.

When the ghost clenched her jaw, the smoke went through the hole that would have been her nose. "Yeah, and caused all kinds of ruckus from what I remember. She must have met him or something because she was head over heels for his crazy ass. I didn't think much of it and believed she would get over it because it seemed quite one-sided." She nodded before she continued.

"But that didn't seem to stop her and it taught me a late lesson—never underestimate what a fool in love will do. She drugged me and the last memory I have of life is the hazy image of Edna holding a large blade over me and candles everywhere. Theatrical moron. I think she tried to bind me to her or that Axman guy but she failed at both. All she was good for was bringing spirits over for quick conversations or making zombies—not that I let her do that often." She frowned. "I saw some on the way here, though. Was that her work? Like one last spell before she died kind of deal?"

Aiyana shook her head. "She died a couple of days ago. I

and a couple of other friends of mine dealt with her zombies then."

"So those sigils in the forest we saw…" Marco began and gestured behind him with his thumb. "I guess they were to stop you?"

"Sigils? What sigils?" Castecka asked.

Aiyana drew one quickly in the dirt. "They looked like barrier sigils to stop a spirit from getting in."

The ghost witch looked at the finished sigil and snorted. "Yeah, it looks like it. But to cover a wide perimeter and keep the illusion up would require considerable phantasma. And if she was still making zombies—"

"And scarecrows," Aiyana interjected. "She was able to make scarecrow-like constructs."

This seemed to surprise the ghost. "Seriously? So maybe she put her nose to the grindstone after she killed me—all over some guy, of course." Her shoulders slumped. "But all that would require great control and considerable phantasma. Even if she started using the books—which she didn't have either—she couldn't have learned that in a matter of a few weeks. Those sigils probably didn't have the juice to work right. I certainly didn't feel anything on the way over."

"I'm guessing you came from the crack in the sky?" Valerie asked.

"Ugh, that's a whole other story," she muttered and took another drag. "I came back only a couple of weeks after I croaked. I had prepared for my eventual demise, even if it happened in a way I didn't expect. The thing is, I had made myself a crossing point to use. I found the Limbo version of it, came over, and was immediately cracked on the head by someone or something and was trapped in a giant skeleton for God knows how long. Then there was a big burst of light and in the next moment, I fell through the sky. It wasn't a big deal, but then this samurai-looking guy pursued me and a few others. I only got away from him about fifteen minutes ago."

"I kind of followed her until the samurai," Marco remarked to Valerie in a low tone.

"Many of those things are connected to the Axman," Aiyana revealed. "He was working with a rogue keeper to break open the veil between life and death."

"The samurai is probably a member of the Wild Hunt," Valerie suggested and finally felt relaxed enough to lower her gun to her side. "Johnny mentioned that they are running around."

"Are they here too?" Castecka sighed. "Things have become rather terrible, haven't they? Maybe I should simply dash off to Limbo and—"

"Wait!" Aiyana interrupted and surprised them all. "Um…I'm sorry, but do you think you can help us?"

"Help you?" the witch asked. "With what exactly?"

The shaman pointed across the field. "We're here because we believe the Axman took our friend to your old house. Your cousin did try to contact him before her death —well, she died because she contacted him, but that's a long story."

Castecka ashed her cigarette. "Does the Axman need your friend for something?"

She nodded. "We believe he needs Annie for his plan to succeed."

The ghost witch considered it for a moment before she

nodded. "I came to get revenge on my cousin but she's not here so I might as well ruin her beau's day while I have the time." She began to float, turned, and headed toward the house. "Hurry along now. We don't have all day!"

Aiyana and Marco began to follow her but Valerie was a little more cautious. "Are we sure we can trust her?"

He shrugged. "She said that she would help us find Annie and she seems to hate the Axman. Both work for me."

The shaman nodded and noticed the familiar rickety shack in the distance. "Well said."

CHAPTER FOURTEEN

"Get the hell off me!" Johnny growled as a shadow he had thought destroyed remained sprawled on the floor but clung to his coat. He aimed his gun down and blasted it in the head. Suddenly free, he tipped back over the pit.

Vic caught him by the collar and pulled him back. "Watch it, kid!" he ordered as he hauled him to his feet. "If you fall, I join you soon after."

"Sorry—look out!" The young detective lifted his gun and fired to strike an oncoming shadow in the chest. His partner turned and fired a shot from the hip that drilled through the top of its skull. "These things are everywhere."

"It's more like they simply won't stay down," the ghost muttered and aimed his gun across the room. "Look over there."

Johnny complied and scowled as a shadow rose slowly from the floor. A few glowing holes in it sealed themselves shut. It looked at them and they fired as one to destroy it as it came back to its unnatural life. "I bet I can guess why they are able to do that."

"We need to take care of Kriminel," Vic stated and looked around the room. "But I don't know where he went exactly."

"It's funny that he talked all that trash and then decided he wanted to play hide and seek." The revenant seethed. "Come out, Kriminel! I thought you wanted to finish this."

"Johnny." They looked up to where several shadows formed quickly above them.

"That wasn't what I meant!" Both partners aimed their weapons and fired to eliminate two of the entities before they even had a chance to form properly. The rest, however, swept toward them screaming, moaning, or making some kind of noise that chilled the young detective to the bone.

They were able to stop their assault but one made it through and swiped at them with long claws. He ducked under the shadow, fired, and blasted it into the barrier around the totem. It writhed against it for a moment before it dissipated and left a small hole in the shield that lasted only a few seconds before it closed. "Vic, did you see that?"

"I'm a little busy, kid," the ghost detective answered as he was slammed into the floor by a shadow that raised a hand holding a dagger. Johnny blasted the weapon out of its hand before it could stab it into his partner. Vic shoved his gun against its head and pulled the trigger several times. He pushed off the floor and through the remains of the terror as it broke apart and then adjusted his jacket. "Okay. Now that's settled, what's up?"

The revenant pointed at the dome. "I blasted one of the shadows into that. It crashed into it and made a hole in the barrier. Although it was small and repaired itself, we can get through."

Vic nodded. "I was able to get my hand in a little and I think if I'd pushed it completely through, it would probably have melted. We'll need to launch a group of these at it to make a large enough opening to get inside without being ripped apart."

"Or maybe we can kill two birds with one stone," Johnny suggested.

Vic tapped his chin and caught onto the idea in moments. "Hmm…maybe, but for that to work, we need to find—"

At a bright flash of red and a scream of rage, they didn't even need to look as their instincts kicked in and they both dove out of the way of a large blast of red energy. They landed at a safe distance and glanced at Kriminel, who was still in his decrepit state but now glowed with red phantasma lining his body like veins. "I have had enough of you interlopers."

"Hey, don't get pissy with us because your brother is better at selecting his chosen ones than you are," Johnny retorted, set the power on his gun to maximum, and charged a shot.

Kriminel growled as he held a hand out toward him and an orb of red phantasma grew within his palm. "I will send you to Hell."

"And I'll send you to get a familial spanking." The revenant fired his shot as the loa launched his attack. The orb pounded into the floor where the young man had been and destroyed it, but Johnny's shot struck his adversary dead center. The disgraced keeper catapulted back into one of the stone pillars before he landed with a loud crash and cracked the foundation.

Vic helped his partner up quickly and they shared a look of surprise, not only that a shot from a simple ether gun had worked but that it had been so effective. "Man, how the mighty have fallen, eh?" the ghost quipped.

"Not far enough yet," Johnny responded and focused on the dome. "You get ready. I'll get him into position so you can rush in and grab the totem."

"Maybe you were right." The ghost detective nodded. "We might not need Samedi after all."

His partner smirked before there was another roar and Kriminel floated higher. "Pats on the back later. Let's get this guy on his ass first." Vic nodded and darted off as the loa pointed an arm at each of them and began to blast them relentlessly.

Johnny evaded the attacks deftly and used the pillars around the room as cover to circle the former keeper. One strike burst a pillar apart and some of the bricks above plummeted to almost crush him. He knew he had to hurry before Kriminel got too pissed off and brought the whole temple down on all of them. While it might work out in their favor, they wouldn't be much good as mush.

He slid, nudged against the side of a staircase, and used it to prop himself up as he aimed at the keeper. "Blast me with your little toy all you want, you pathetic child!" Kriminel growled, his focus now completely on him as Vic came out of hiding and crossed the room quickly. "I may be weakened but you are a fool if you believe you have the power to destroy me."

"I hope I don't, to be honest," the young detective

muttered and held the trigger down. "But I hope you have enough power to destroy yourself." He fired and the shot launched their adversary toward the dome. Hope soared along with Kriminel, but the loa held his arms out and stopped himself mere inches before he powered into the barrier.

"You fool!" he roared and shadows began to form around the room again. "That is the last shot you will land on me."

"You're right," Vic responded and hurled himself at the loa. "My turn now!" He slammed into him and they drove into the barrier. Kriminel uttered a cry of pain and the shadows he was making began to break apart.

The two combatants pushed through the barrier. Whatever resembled the loa's flesh began to peel apart and red mist-like phantasma flowed from him as the ghost used him as a shield. Vic snagged the totem within quickly as their momentum carried them through the center. Kriminel's cry intensified as they continued out the other side and crash-landed beyond the pit.

Johnny yanked his jacket off and extended his arm. "Vic, give it here!" he shouted. His partner tossed him the totem before their adversary kicked him in the side and launched him into the wall.

The loa stood with a grimace. The entire rear of his body and parts of his left side were torn open and he tried to repair himself as he hobbled forward and formed another blast. "Don't you dare!"

The revenant caught the totem and lifted his jacket as Kriminel fired. Vic could only watch helplessly with bright eyes as the blast connected and a bright red glow engulfed his partner. Once it began to fade, however, the young man was still standing with another, larger figure in front of him.

That figure began to chuckle teasingly. "Oh, that tickled." Kriminel stood frozen, his shaking hands balled into fists. The red light finally subsided to reveal Baron Samedi and the very temple itself seemed to respond to its master's return. As all the torches in the room and down the halls lit and the destruction around the room began to repair itself.

The keeper walked forward and stood in front of his brother. Seeing the two side by side encapsulated the difference between them now. The purple baron stood several feet taller than his brother and his body was strong and taut compared to the other loa's almost zombie-like look.

"It's good to see you again brother," Samedi said although the expression on his face made it seem like he was anything but pleased. He snaked his arm out, snatched Kriminel by the throat, and lifted him to meet his eyes. "For the last time."

"Get to the hold!" Rick shouted as he and Donovan dodged another swipe of the undine's tail. "Get to the hold!"

"You've yelled that this whole time," the agent replied and fired a shot at the terror as he bounded down a flight of stairs. "I've got the picture."

"Then why aren't you doing it harder?" the mobster demanded as he blasted a veritable barrage from his machine gun.

Donovan noticed a large door at the end of the hall. "We're almost there. You know, if your explosives were a little more potent, we would have help right now."

In response, the mobster lobbed his last piece of spectral dynamite at the undine before he slid down the stairs. The terror shrieked as it detonated. He turned and poked a boney finger into his companion's chest.

"Oh yeah, the almighty agent with all the fancy gadgets wants to shame me for our arsenal. I don't see you offering anything with a little more oomph! What's your excuse?" They turned at a gurgling noise and scowled when the water that was falling down the stairs began to ascend as the terror put itself together again. "Son of a bitch!"

"Come on. We'll yell at each other later," the agent suggested as they rushed to the door.

Rick stopped in front of it. "Hmm…the magnetic lock is still on." He looked questioningly at the man beside him. "It's not an issue for me but can you get through?"

Donovan took a small circular device out and placed it on the door. It beeped four times before a green light went off and was followed by a click and a hiss. He took it off the door and it began to open. "Fancy gadgets, right?"

The mobster rolled his eyes as the undine shrieked in fury. "Man, that bitch suddenly wants all the attention, huh?" he grumbled as they entered a massive space filled with boxes of cargo.

"Shit, what are we looking for?" the agent asked as the ghost had already begun to search boxes by simply phasing his head through them.

"A big-ass gun," Rick replied as he floated up a stack of five crates and looked into the top one.

Donovan noticed the undine coming toward them and slammed the door shut quickly before he put the device on to lock it. "You're the mob. You mostly deal in big-ass guns."

"Well, yeah, but I gotta find the fuckers."

The undine slammed into the other side of the door. "Maybe I can help search. What color crate is it in?"

"Red!" the ghost shouted as he looked into another stack.

The agent took stock and scowled. "There are dozens of red ones. Wouldn't a special gun get its own crate?"

"On the inside, yeah. What? Do you think we would carry a seriously illegal weapon in a golden crate lined with jewels or something?"

"Everything in here is probably illegal."

Rick stopped for a moment and considered this. "Also true."

Donovan cursed under his breath when he saw water pouring through the door. "The door is leaking."

The ghost took out the baton the agent had given him. "It probably wasn't housebroken properly. But if it's the snake, use this."

He tossed it to the man, who pressed the button to lengthen it. "If you are going to regift something to someone, it is usually a different person." The water on the ground began to form into the head of the undine.

"Quips later, jackass! Hold that bitch off until I find what we need," Rick ordered as he disappeared into the back of the room.

The agent ran up to the undine, thrust the baton into its forehead, and pressed the switch to electrocute it. The terror's expressionless face suddenly transformed into that of an angered snake-like woman and it hissed in rage. Its body convulsed but didn't break apart. He backed away and began to fire as the entity wound a tentacle around the baton and removed it from its head before it shattered the device.

It then lashed out at the agent as he fired. He dodged most of the strikes as he retreated but one caught him in the shin and upended him, and his gun tumbled out of his grasp. It was snagged immediately by another tentacle and destroyed in moments. He scowled as he drew his pistol, checked his ammo, and selected several teal-colored bullets.

Once they were loaded into the weapon, he fired at the terror. They landed and ethereal ice began to form on the creature, but cracks manifested quickly. The undine's watery form poured through them and it reshaped itself instead of simply trying to break the ice.

Donovan wasted no time and tried to get some distance between it and him. He scuttled deeper into the hold and looked around for Rick, although he didn't want to shout for him and give his position away if the terror had lost him.

Fortunately, the ghost found him instead. "What are you doing back here?" he asked and startled the agent, who almost blasted him in response.

"Getting away from the undine."

"You failed to stop it and I'm caught up," the mobster responded and his companion rolled his eyes. "It's good you are here, anyway. I found the cannon—almost all the way in the back, of course. I need your help to fire it."

"Why?"

"It's a big honker," Rick explained as they hurried to the back of the hold.

"Can't you simply possess it and fire it that way?" Donovan asked.

The ghost looked over his shoulder. "What part of big do you not understand? We might be able to possess nonliving things but there is a limit to how much weight."

"You can possess the living too."

Rick fixed him with a mocking grin. "Yeah, sure. The agent points out what creepy bastards ghosts are. We can't do it all the time and I won't give you a gold star for trivia." He pointed ahead to a group of crates hidden from the rest, one of the red ones already open. "That one."

They reached the crate. Donovan looked inside and his eyes widened. "What the hell is this?" he asked. The massive weapon looked like a combination of a cannon and a rocket launcher.

When the undine shrieked, much closer now, they knew it was approaching fast. "I'll give you an explanation later," Rick stated as he reached in and began to pull the back end out. "Help me to get this ready."

The agent took the front half and they struggled to pull it out. They placed it on the floor and the ghost flipped a few switches and turned a couple of knobs.

It began to glow with a dark-blue light. "This looks like something we're developing at the Agency."

"Yeah, well, the Chinese beat you to it. Assuming it works," Rick added as he tilted it up.

"You don't know?"

"I haven't had a chance to use it yet. Getting things off

the black market from the other side of the planet is a fickle thing." There was a loud splash and they saw the undine slip itself between stacks of crates. "The fat lady is warmed up. It's time to see if she can sing." He hoisted the back end on his shoulder. "I got to hold this switch down to keep the charge from shorting out so you get to fire."

Donovan took the front end quickly and shouldered it like a bazooka. He slid his finger into the trigger. "It needs to charge the shot so hold the trigger down for a few seconds," the mobster instructed as the undine saw them and revealed its watery fangs again. He pressed down on the trigger and heard a loud buzz as the chamber of the weapon began to spin and a large orb formed inside.

They tensed as the terror surged toward them, sending out tendrils that seemed ready to pierce through them instead of capture them.

"Anytime now!" Rick shouted. The agent released the trigger and the shot fired and hurled both of them on their asses as it plowed into the undine. A shockwave of energy ran through it and it uttered one final gasped shriek before it vanished from sight and didn't even leave any water behind.

The agent managed to sit, breathless and sore, but a smile formed on his face as he turned to look at his companion. "It looks like a successful test, huh?" He laughed before he noticed the ghost was unmoving. "Rick?" He crawled closer and noticed that the mobster's glow had faded. His hands and the side of his face were a dull gray, the symptoms of ether poisoning. "Rick!" he shouted and tried to grasp one of his hands but his went right through them.

With an almost inaudible moan, the mobster stirred and pointed weakly to his jacket. Enough of his phantasma remained that it was still tangible and Donovan opened it, dug hastily in the pocket, and retrieved a vial of stygia. He popped it open and poured it on the ghost, whose color returned as he managed to sit slowly.

"Man, that bitch can sing, huh?" he muttered as his companion helped him up.

"I guess there was ether in the blowback?" the agent asked and studied the weapon. "I could have taken the back end."

"I didn't have the time to think of the effects." The ghost's eyes brightened as he looked at the cannon. "Shit, we didn't break it, did we?"

"I don't think so." Donovan was about to follow when Rick went to inspect it but received a notification in his helmet. He answered the call from Anderson. "Report, Agent."

"We've finished off the drowned up here, sir," she replied matter of factly. "With no casualties. How are things on your end?"

He walked to the place where the undine was destroyed. "The terror has been dealt with." He noted how dry the area was. "One hundred percent confirmed on that. We're in the hold and found the weapon we came here for."

"Roger. What do you need us to do?"

Donovan thought about it and turned to Rick. "Our team finished off the drowned. Do you think we're ready to head back?"

The mobster nodded. "Yeah. I'll have some of my men come down to get this back in its box and make sure everything is accounted for. Me and the rest will go and get Sully and whoever he needs of the crew in here to get the vessel to harbor." He pointed at the other crates. "If you want, feel free to take a look around and see what kind of goods we're packing."

He looked at the cannon and wondered what else could be hiding in the crates. "I appreciate it. If command asks, I'll simply say we found these floating at sea."

Rick rolled his eyes. "Ha-ha. Make sure they remember we're playing nice for now."

The agent opened his comms again. "Anderson, we're coming back. Prepare the rest of the team to finish their sweep. The ghosts will take care of the ship."

"Understood. See you soon," she replied and the comms went silent again.

Donovan caught up with the waiting ghost. "So what do we do once we reach New Orleans again?"

"I thought we already had a plan."

"And that was?"

Rick held his gun up. "When we get back, it's open season on that bastard the Axman."

CHAPTER FIFTEEN

"Oh, my Lord, this place is a wreck!" Castecka fumed as they wandered into the shack.

Marco looked around with a grimace. "Yeah, yeah, it could use some spit shining." He looked at her. "You got any secret rooms or anything around here? Someplace the Axman could have hidden my sister?"

The ghost witch frowned as she stared at piles of wax on a cracked table and long-dried bloodstains. "Oh, sure. A few. There's one over there by the grandfather clo—." She stopped when she saw it torn down. "I guess that one is not so secret."

"It is not," Aiyana replied as she ascended the stairs. "She is not there. Moreover, I cannot sense her here."

"Dammit!" Marco growled and swung his bat into the kitchen counter. "Sorry. I can pay for that."

Castecka waved him off. "It's not like I'll stay here now anyway. Besides, you might not be able to feel her presence because it is blocked and I know what might be doing it." She floated to the master bedroom and stood in front of one of the mirrors, although it didn't reflect her form. "My meditation room is where I would usually practice my sigils and something like a phantasma dampener is easy to maintain, especially if you use some stygian candles to keep it going."

She felt around the edges of the mirror and clicked two buttons. It slid away and revealed another passage into the basement.

The group wandered in and hurried through the dark passage until they saw a dim light at the other end that suggested the flickering of candles. They entered a mostly barren room with numerous sigils and a few pillows here and there. At the edge of the room next to a furnace, a young woman slept on the floor.

"Annie!" Marco shouted and ran to her with Valerie.

"Huh?" she muttered and stirred in her sleep. "Marco? Marco!" She gasped when her brother embraced her. "You're here. I can't believe it!"

"Believe it, sis," he reassured her as Valerie took a knife out and began to cut the ropes binding her. "You aren't hurt, are you?"

She shook her head. "No, I'm all right. I'm all right now."

Castecka looked at them with a slight smile. "Thank you," the shaman said softly.

The ghost shrugged as she took a drag from her holder. "I didn't exactly expect a happy ending when I came but it is quite nice." She tilted her head as she stared at the wall. "What's this?" she asked as she floated closer.

Aiyana followed her and frowned at a large series of sigils in the wall. "It's not one of your projects?"

The witch shook her head. "Not at all. From the looks of this, it appears to be an advanced form of necromancy. I've dabbled in it, of course, but this seems to be an attempt to give a ghost a corporeal body."

"The Axman is attempting to resurrect himself," Aiyana explained. "This could have been one of his methods."

"A very foolish one," Castecka noted snidely. "This would simply allow a ghost to have a more human form, not an actual one. Not only would it not last all that long, but to get this to work in the first place would require an immense amount of phantasma and stygia and at least a dozen powerful spirit callers to even have a decent chance to work."

"A more human form?" the shaman asked and studied the series of glyphs. "What could he be trying to accomplish with that?"

With a shrug, the ghost gestured at the sigils. "It beats me. You would probably have a better chance at finding answers than I would," she admitted. "What this would accomplish would be akin to making a zombie. But the reason zombies act so...well, zombie-like is because the connection is always rather rough. This would be more direct and create a body the ghost could inhabit and still retain all their mental functions and physical control."

"The Axman did something similar with his followers," Valerie recalled as she joined them. "But their bodies would decay and they needed a victim to use to begin with."

"That's more a full possession. It's still as impressive as it is macabre but wouldn't have the same benefits as this would. This body would decay quickly but you couldn't distinguish it from an actual living being for a time." The witch turned and floated toward Annie. "Excuse me, do you have a moment?"

The siblings broke from their embrace to look at her. "Uh…hello." Annie looked confused. "I'm sorry but who are you?"

"A previous tenant," she responded glibly and ashed her cigarette "But more importantly, a witch. Did this Axman give you any clues as to what he wanted you for?" She pointed to the sigils. "What those might be for?"

The woman frowned and approached the wall to look for herself. "He said he needed me to break the veil—that I was his key." She grimaced and looked at the others. "He said something like I would be his mother."

"Mother?" Castecka asked and her eyes dimmed. "Oh… my God."

"What is it?" Valerie asked.

The ghost witch shook her head. "That is disgusting but it might work."

"What would?" Marco demanded.

"He got his metaphors mixed up." She looked at Annie. "You aren't his key, you are his key*hole* if you catch my meaning." She shuddered. "If he has the ability to make that sigil work, he can give himself a body that is no different from a living one—specifically a human male. He would still technically be a ghost but one that had all the proper equipment." She looked at each member of the group. "He intended to literally make her his mother and have her make him a new body. If he succeeded, he would, technically, be reborn."

It seemed to take them slightly different lengths of time

to grasp her meaning, but all reacted with horror and disgust.

"What the fuck?" Marco yelled. "Can he do that?"

"Quite possibly," Castecka replied. "If he's trying to break the veil...well, think about more scientific laws. If you found a waterfall running upward, that would essentially disprove the law of gravity, right? If you can find a way to truly resurrect a ghost, that would break down the laws of life and death—and I don't want to think of the repercussions of that."

"But why does he need Annie for that?" Marco demanded. "Look, I know this sounds horrible, but couldn't he simply use any woman for that?"

"It's because of your family's connection to Anne Schneider," Aiyana reminded them as she looked at the witch. "They are descendants of one of his victims from a century ago. Not only did she survive but she had a child right after the attack."

"I see...that could be an explanation," she muttered. "I have no idea if this could even truly work but our connections are precious to us as ghosts. There was a saying even before the veil loosened that every person dies twice. Once when they are alive and again when everyone forgets about them. Now it is a little more literal, but it is true that once everyone on the living side forgets a person's existence, their connection to life weakens. But an event like that would be powerful and one of the few things a rat like the Axman can cling to—along with his infamy, I suppose. Using a vessel with that kind of connection would probably be his best bet at achieving his goal."

Annie wrapped her arms tightly around herself. "Does

he think I would simply accept it? That I wouldn't…deal with the child?"

"I don't think he would have given you a choice," Castecka replied. "He would probably simply possess the child after he watched over you while you carried it. Or who knows? Maybe a ghost baby has a fast birth cycle. It's not something I want to think about either way and I'm sure it isn't something you want to experience either."

Marco moved to comfort his sibling. "And you won't have to. Let's get you out of here, Annie."

Suddenly, both Castecka and Aiyana looked toward one of the walls. "Something is coming," the shaman warned.

"I have a bad feeling I know who," the ghost witch added and moved quickly to one of the shelves and snatched a large vase and a black stick.

"We need to go!" Valerie shouted and the group ran out of the room and into the shack. They had barely made it out the door when they heard a shout of rage.

"Where are you!" the Axman roared as the group ran into the field.

"Follow me," Castecka ordered as she darted left. They complied and entered a large circular clearing. The witch held the stick up and it floated from her hand and lowered to begin to make etchings in the dirt. "Steer clear for a moment," she instructed as she opened the vase and poured the stygia all around her body. Her hair grew more volume and green skin appeared on her. "I can teleport us out of here but I'll need a moment."

In the distance, the shack was blown apart. The Axman floated in the air, now back to his dark, giant form. "Annie!" he cried as he searched the fields.

"I'm not sure we can give you that!" Marco stated as he held his bat up and the blue phantasma flames encircled it.

"We will." Aiyana took out two wolf figurines and tossed them on the ground. The forms of ghostly wolves grew from them and snarled. The Axman's gaze finally settled on the group and shades appeared around him as he flew directly at them.

Valerie stepped forward and fired. Her shots dealt with the shades easily as the wolves howled and leapt at the Axman. He swatted one away but the other bit his arm while the first recovered and sank its spectral teeth into his leg. With a growl, he kicked it off of him and ripped the other off his arm.

He lifted his ax to end it when a burst of white flame blasted him, followed by Valerie hitting him with ether bullets. Marco came up from the side and swung his bat into the side of his head.

All these attacks were for naught, however.

The bat barely staggered the killer and the bullets and flames didn't seem to unnerve him at all. He walked through the fire as one of the wolves leapt at him. Casually, he took hold of it and slammed it on the ground, stamped on it, and broke the figurine within so it disappeared. The other wolf tried to attack from behind but he simply tossed his ax and cleaved it in two before the weapon spun toward Marco, who rolled under it as it continued its journey to land in the Axman's hand.

"How much longer?" Valerie asked as Castecka placed her hands on the dirt.

"I need a destination—come here," she ordered. Valerie and Annie complied quickly as Aiyana and Marco tried to slow the Axman. "Give me your arm and think of a destination," she said and the officer held hers out. The witch caught hold of it. "We need to go now!"

"Go, Marco!" Aiyana shouted as she dug another totem out.

He ran past her. "What about you?"

"I'll make sure he can't follow us." A shadow loomed over her and she gasped when she was knocked off her feet. the Axman towered over her, covered in her white flames.

"Aiyana!" Valerie cried and attempted to leave the circle.

The shaman turned and created a barrier of flame in front of Marco and the others. "Go and save Annie! I got this." She turned and raised her hand but the killer's ax buried itself in her chest.

"Aiyana!" her friends cried as their forms began to become translucent.

"You have nothing, shaman!" The Axman sneered as he yanked his ax out and approached her friends.

Weakly, Aiyana snagged the back of his leg. "I have you," she whispered and held her blood-soaked totem up as he looked back. There was a flash of green light and he roared as he tried to lurch toward the others before he disappeared. Her friends vanished.

When the Axman landed, he felt a mighty pull against him that dragged him back. He slammed his ax into the ground as he was almost yanked off his feet. Grimly, he forced himself to march forward and used his ax to pull him along a crumbling street until he was far enough away to look around at the crumbling medieval and Native American architecture that surrounded him. He looked back at a massive dark void that drew in the debris around him. As he pressed forward again, he cursed the shaman with each step until he was finally far enough away from the Big Dark that he didn't feel its pull.

That damn girl. Was this the best she could do as a parting insult? If she thought she had trapped him in Limbo she was gravely mistaken. He was so close—so damn close—to achieving his plan. But he had his power back now and even though he could feel it slipping from him, he still had time. There were only so many places the others could hide. He would find them and he would take the girl back.

A moment later, he sensed something familiar. It was weak and he didn't know exactly where it was, but he knew this feeling. If he were in a better mood, he might have laughed. It seemed that the shaman's plan had worked out for him. At least now he wouldn't have to worry about the ticking clock and he could tie up a loose end. He proceeded down the street and reached out for the connection he thought he'd lost. It appeared that it was merely hiding from him. Of course he couldn't sense it in the living world. What connections did that loa have there now anyway?

Soon, he would have the power.

CHAPTER SIXTEEN

"Do you think this is it?" Kriminel demanded and spat at Samedi's feet. "You will simply spend eternity as someone else's lackey? You would kill your own family rather than seize greatness?"

The baron frowned and kicked his brother's feet out from under him. He extended a hand and it filled with purple energy. "You know the answer to that, brother," he chided and almost spat the last word in disgust. "Otherwise, you would have come to me to begin with."

"I always knew you were weak. That was why I knew I could not depend on you, Samedi!" Kriminel seethed, only to be backhanded by his fellow loa.

Vic looked on with apathy as Johnny winced. "Damn, you know that hurt."

The ghost detective shrugged. "I've never been one for this Shakespearean dramatic crap. I want to get out of here and have a cigarette. Whatever Samedi plans to do, I wish he would do it before something else goes wrong."

"Then why don't you go tell him to wrap it up?"

There was a flash of purple light and the room shook. Kriminel cried out as he crashed into a stone wall and slumped again. Vic craned his head. "It looks like he's having a moment. I don't think I should bother him."

The revenant smothered a snicker. "It's probably the smarter move."

Samedi stormed up to his brother, who tried wearily to stand. The baron grasped him by the throat and lifted him off his feet. "I know this must end, brother. You have crossed a line and there is no way to fix this." His hand began to glow. "And you know how it will end."

Kriminel attempted to spit at him again, but he simply tightened his hold around his throat and he croaked in response. "I hope you look forward to your eternity as nothing more than a pet," he growled. "I know that one day, you will see that I was right, brother! And when that day comes you will regret—" His head snapped up and although he continued to stare, he didn't seem to be looking at his brother. "Oh ho ho. So you finally made yourself useful, huh?"

The partners drew their guns. "Is someone here?" Vic asked and glanced at the baron.

"I don't feel anything." Samedi shook his brother. "Is this some desperate trick?"

Kriminel ignored him. "Where are you? What good are you to me over—wait! What are you doing? You are nothing without—agh!" He began to flail in Samedi's grasp and the lights in his eyes vanished. The loa thrust his hand quickly into Kriminel's chest and the body fell limp against him. He bowed his head and lowered his hand. His brother's corpse fell, shrank quickly, and shriveled.

The partners ran up. "What the hell was that, Baron?" the ghost detective demanded as he looked at Kriminel's body. "Is he gone?"

Samedi nodded grimly. "What remained of his spirit—his life— is gone. Kriminel no longer exists as a loa or an entity at all but his essence..." He turned and looked at them. "The remnants of his power were no longer there when I ended him."

Johnny shared a confused look with his partner. "And that means what exactly?"

"That someone took it. Whoever my brother talked to in his final moments." He folded his arms. "It's not something one can do easily, even in Kriminel's pathetic condition. Either there is a powerful unknown player in all this or we all know who took it."

"The Axman." Johnny growled and almost turned and drove his fist into a wall before Vic stopped him. "Dammit. How the hell did he even do that?"

"They had a bond with each other like we do," the ghost detective reminded him. "But with Kriminel weakened, I guess the Axman thought he would simply take what he needed and leave him to rot."

"But why now?" the revenant demanded. "Something must have happened. Otherwise, you would think he would have done it after the portal opened."

Samedi held a hand out and a portal opened in front of them. "We will find out soon," he stated and gestured at the gateway. "Let us return to New Orleans."

"Are you coming too?" Vic asked.

The baron nodded. "I need to close that tear to the path.

And if the Axman does have whatever remains of my brother…well, I need to claim it."

Johnny allowed himself a small grin. "It looks like the Axman screwed himself."

"It depends on what we find when we get back," Vic replied and fused with him. "Let's go, partner." The young detective nodded as he and Samedi stepped through the portal and appeared on the same hotel rooftop they had left from to go to the baron's realm.

Johnny looked over the edge and noticed scattered groups of people on other rooftops as well as broken windows, cars on the street, and a few ghosts who floated about. "Man, there'll be so much to fix after this is all over," he muttered as his partner reappeared.

The ghost detective nodded. "It certainly takes strong folk to live here. Although hopefully, New Orleans won't have to deal with another swarm of terrors and a crack in the sky any time soon."

The revenant scratched his head. "Maybe they can make it a tourist attraction if it happens again."

Vic looked at him with a dour expression. "What the hell is wrong with you?"

"That can all be decided later," the baron interrupted from where he floated above them. "For now, I should tend to this mess first."

He flew quickly to the portal and held his palms out. Purple light formed around the edges of the crack and Samedi began to draw his hands toward each other. The portal began to close and when Johnny looked around, almost everyone stared at the sky.

It would be too much of a coincidence for all of them to

be specters, so it meant that all this time, the entire population could see the anomaly. He wondered how that had made them feel. Those who could not regularly see ghosts unless they were charged with stygia had to deal with this big-ass tear in the sky and the destruction the escaped terrors wrought even if they could not see them.

There would probably be a few who chose to move out of the city after this was all said and done.

"You there!" a booming voice shouted. Johnny and Vic looked at three huntsmen who floated down to them, two in African dress and another in samurai armor. "You are the two who alerted us to the matter with Kriminel."

The revenant nodded. "Yeah, I remember you. I don't think I caught your name, though."

"I am Kaitō." The samurai-like warrior looked at the portal that had now shrunk to less than half the size. "Baron Samedi returns and he's closing the break. At least that's two problems taken care of."

"How go the hunts?" Vic questioned and patted his jacket. "And do any of you have a smoke?"

He appeared to be out of luck. The two African huntsmen shook their heads and Kaitō simply ignored his last question. "There are still terrors about, not to mention rogue ghosts. But it is not only us in the fight. The living and the ghost mafia have also dealt with them." He bowed his head and looked at the other warriors. "Unfortunately, we have also suffered losses as well." He revealed broken pieces of armor and Johnny's eyes widened when he saw a familiar helm and dark phantasma. "That's...that's Viking's helmet isn't it?" he asked. "Was he obliterated?"

Kaitō nodded grimly. "He and two other noble huntsmen. No simple terror could have felled three huntsmen." He pointed to the dark phantasma. "And from what I have gathered about the monster who stalks this city, I believe that is his calling card?"

"More like his refuse," Vic muttered as he shoved hands in his pockets and scowled. "I had been told that he lost his powers after his connection with Kriminel was severed."

"It appears he drained our brothers' phantasma to reignite those dark powers," one of the other huntsmen explained. "He has some ability to drain our very essence. I do not know how he is able to do this."

"It must be a power granted to him by the corrupt loa," the other suggested.

The samurai folded his arms. "Still, it is unnatural, even compared to what we are used to. However, if any fortune can come of this, it means he will lose that power at some point without his master to call upon."

The ghost detective looked up slowly. "About that...I don't think we are so fortunate."

All the huntsmen turned to him. "What are you talking about?"

"Johnny, Vic!" Samedi called and floated down to them. The lights in his eyes glimmered slightly when he saw the new arrivals. "Huntsmen," he greeted with a nod as he landed on the roof. "How has your day been?"

Kaitō looked at the loa. Although the keeper might have been at least two feet taller and more powerful than he was, he showed no fear or reverence. "It's been busy, Keeper. We could have used your assistance much sooner."

Samedi rolled his shoulders and nodded apologetically. "Yes, and I do apologize for that. It appears my brother was much more crafty than I suspected—a foolish mistake on my part given all he has accomplished thus far. But it will not be a problem from here on."

"So the disgrace has been taken care of?" one of the other warriors asked.

The baron nodded before he looked out at the city. "Yes, he will trouble no one from here on. But that does not mean the darkness has lifted. The Axman is still out there."

Kaitō looked at the city with him. "True, but without the assistance of your kin, he will not be much more trouble now, will he?"

Vic stepped forward. "That's what I was getting to," he stated. The samurai looked over his shoulder at him. "You see, just before Kriminel died, he babbled like he was talking to someone. Then, he thrashed about and shriveled like an old prune. We...uh, think the Axman has taken what remained of his power."

"What?" Kaitō demanded and turned to Samedi. "How could you let that happen?"

"Hey, man, it caught us all off guard," Johnny interjected. "We didn't even know it was possible or how he did it. You would think if he could do it all along, he would have done it long before now and spared Vic and me a road trip through a big-ass graveyard and creepy jungle." His gaze snapped to Samedi, who adjusted his jacket before he coughed into his fist. "No offense, baron."

The loa held a hand up. "None taken. My style of decoration is an...acquired taste, I admit." He turned to the huntsman. "But you are right. Much of this rests on my shoulders and that is why I am here to make it right." He looked at the sky where the tear used to be. "At least we have one problem resolved. As long as no new ones spring up, I believe we can resolve everything soon enough."

"Hey." Vic pointed far into the horizon of the city. "Do you guys see that shimmer?" The group peered out and located it easily enough. More importantly, they saw it grow until it rose high above even the tallest building in the city and began to expand. Johnny looked behind him and saw another wall form on the other side of the city and stretch to meet the first one in the middle.

"What is going on?" Kaitō asked and scowled as the barrier began to seal around the city.

The revenant gritted his teeth. "The Agency," he muttered before he saw Vic leaning over out of the corner of his eye. "Hey, are you feeling all right?"

The ghost detective looked like he wanted to nod before he shook his head quickly. "I…uh, feel a little woozy kid." As soon as he said it, Johnny was also swamped by a wave of nausea. That was normal, but how did a ghost get sick?

CHAPTER SEVENTEEN

In one moment, Valerie stood in a field and watched her friend try to hold the Axman off. A moment later, she was in front of her precinct, surrounded by the remains of the chaos that had broken out only hours earlier. She pushed to her feet and looked around. "Wait—what?"

"It's a little disorienting at first, dear," Castecka told her, adjusted her hair, and dug in her purse. "Teleportation always is, especially when the living are involved." She lit a cigarette without a holder this time. "It explains why it fell out of practice for most so long ago. Now, it's more of a ghost thing."

"Val…" Marco whispered and placed a hand on her shoulder. "Are you all right?"

Annie pushed to her feet and took a moment to get her head straight. Tears filled her eyes. "Aiyana…" She looked at the officer. "I'm so sorry, Valerie."

She fought her tears although her body tried to resist and she shook her head. "She gave us a chance to escape so we could end this." Her voice was slightly hoarse as she rubbed her eyes. "I know I'll see her again. She promised as much. I'll grieve later and let her relatives know that she died fighting. But I also want to let them know that it wasn't in vain." She looked at the siblings. "Let's make sure the next time we see the Axman that it will be the last, all right?"

They nodded. She wiped her eyes on her sleeve again before she turned to the ghost. "Thank you for your help."

Castecka nodded with as much of a reassuring smile as she could muster. "Well, we may have just met but the fact that you are trying to obliterate that bastard the Axman certainly got you on my good side rather quickly." She took a drag. "I am sorry about your friend. Whenever I get back, I'll look for her. Limbo can be very overwhelming for newcomers."

Valerie responded with a small smile. "Thank you. When I come up with the right words, I'll have you pass a message along as well if you don't mind."

"Not at all," she agreed readily. "But until then, do you have a plan?"

The officer looked at the precinct. "I need a sit-rep. I don't know what has happened since we've been gone and we need to inform everyone that the Axman is back to full strength as far as we know." The siblings nodded as she regarded the ghost witch. "I know this is a lot to ask, especially with everything going on, but do you mind tagging along for a while longer?"

Castecka chuckled. "It's been a while since anyone wanted my company. Is there something I can do?"

"I'm not completely sure of what you are capable of. But with Aiyana gone, the only other spirit caller I know is a voodoo priestess who focuses more on the spirituality and healing side of things and…" She shrugged.

"You need someone who has a few bullets in the chamber?" the witch finished and took another drag with a chuckle. She touched her face as her ethereal skin began to fade. "Well, I would certainly be pleased to help obliterate my sycophantic cousin's crush but that teleportation spell took quite a lot out of me. I'm willing to stay a while and listen but I'll need more stygia."

The officer nodded and gestured toward the building. "I have a private stash. I can get you refreshed but I need to talk to the chief first."

Castecka crushed the cigarette in her hand and let it float to a nearby trash can. "Then lead the way, darling." The Maggio siblings nodded and Valerie turned and headed inside.

While outside wasn't exactly tranquil, it was a hell of a lot better than inside. The precinct wasn't as panicked as it had been when the tear opened but dozens of people still raced about. Many citizens were also present, either trying to get information or looking for a place of refuge.

The group walked past it all and the officer noticed several people look at her. They seemed surprised to see she had brought yet another ghost in, but some also looked relieved that she had Annie with her.

She approached Shemar's office and knocked. "Come in!" The reply was quick but weary. When she opened the door, her commander huddled over his computer, numerous files, and two whiteboards with various messages and information stuck to it. "Officer Simone, did you—" He stopped when he saw Annie. "Oh, thank God. Are you okay, Miss Maggio?"

Annie nodded. "I'm all right. But the Axman attacked us and we lost…" The words drifted off and she pursed her lips.

Shemar looked at the group. "Aiyana isn't here?" He focused on Valerie. "So she's…oh… Valerie, I'm sorry. I know you worked with her on several occasions and—"

"It's all right, sir. I'll mourn her after I avenge her," she stated, her tone strong but curt with the strain of keeping it together. "But I need to let you know that the Axman seems to have his powers back in full. We were only able to escape with the help of Castecka here." She gestured to the witch, who gave the police chief a casual wave.

Shemar nodded. "Thank you for looking after my officer and her friends," he told her before he looked at Valerie. "As for the Axman…that's trouble, Simone. I was told the mob had a run-in with him earlier and he still managed to escape without those damn powers of his. But they were at least able to beat him back. If he's returned full of piss and vinegar, that might tip the scales. Lovett has itched to activate that dome of theirs since they got here but for the past hour, she's been very insistent."

"How's the situation with the terrors and aggressive ghosts?"

He closed a few files. "It's improved. We've rounded up a good number of ghosts who were causing trouble with the supernatural population or simply being menaces in general and have them in ether cells. The huntsmen and the mob have mostly dealt with the terrors. Fortunately, we haven't heard anything about the Wild Hunt turning on the mob or general populace so they are at least keeping their eyes where they need to be for now. The terrors are dwindling but they could have simply found haunts and are hiding for the time being." He sighed and rubbed his forehead. "Even when the immediate threat is over, this will have long-lasting repercussions. There will be many long days in the future."

Castecka shrugged. "I believe the saying is 'There's always something going down in New Orleans.' It's part of the reason I moved here."

"You moved here because of the ghosts?" he asked. "To be around a community like yourself?"

"Oh, I was alive until a couple of months ago." She sat in a chair in the corner of the office. "I won't go through the whole story again but I have my reasons to take care of the Axman. I'm a witch by profession. Your officer believes I might be of some help."

Shemar frowned and looked at Valerie. "Officer, I know these are desperate circumstances but should we involve citizens?" He looked at Castecka. "Even relatively unique ones?"

She folded her arms. "Yes, sir. It's not traditional at all but like you said, desperate times. I am not completely sure of what we have to do to deal with the Axman, but having options would be valuable."

The chief considered this for a moment. "You do know the risks, correct?"

Castecka nodded and crossed one leg over the other. "Oh yes. I've had a good look at him. He is a demonic-looking son of a bitch but any fear he might strike in me is countered by how much I want to kill him." She tilted her head from side to side for a moment. "Well, obliterate him, but you get the point."

He sighed and looked briefly at Valerie again before he focused on the witch. "Will you return to Limbo once this is over?"

"I don't have any other reason to stay."

Shemar shrugged and stood. "Very well. We will need to discuss your abilities and training but for now, we'll keep you as a retainer. If you can assist us in the future, we would be grateful."

"Marvelous," Castecka responded flatly but with a small smile. "Now can I have some of that stygia, dear?"

Valerie nodded and pointed through the door. "My office is on the other side of the room. It says Officer Valerie Simone on the door so you can't miss it. I have five vials in the third drawer down on the left. Will that suffice?"

The witch floated up and nodded. "Certainly—for now. But if you need another grand display like in the fields, I'll need quite a few more."

"If it comes to that, I'll make sure you get it," she promised as the ghost turned transparent and floated through the door. She turned to the chief. "You guys haven't had a chance to make a plan since I've been gone have you?"

He almost rolled his eyes. "Besides the barrier, the Agency still seems to want to drop their bomb on our city."

"Bomb?" Marco scowled. "Like a nuke? What? They don't want the Axman to have anyone to kill so they will simply kill everyone instead?"

"It's not that type of bomb," Valerie assured him but she folded her arms tightly. "Not that it makes it much better."

"Either way, they sure as hell won't drop anything," Shemar stated firmly. He leaned back in his chair. "But to answer your question, no, we don't. We had sent teams out to find him and finish him since he was in a weakened state. But if he's back to full strength, that complicates things a hell of a lot. I need to arrange another meeting with all the parties but the only way I can see this ending is with his obliteration—or we find some way to trap him."

"Maybe we should lead him to the Wild Hunt?" Valerie suggested. "I would consider killing two birds in this case. They've played ball for now but who knows if it'll stay that way. I doubt the ghost mafia running around will please them either."

"I could help." Annie offered and stepped forward. "My power—my empath or whatever it is—can hurt him but I can't control it properly right now." She looked at her brother. "Marco, maybe you can teach me while they hunt him."

He frowned and looked at his bat. "In a few hours? I should mention that I just got you back and I'm not keen to throw you into danger again. That said, don't you remember how long it took Dad and me to get this under control?"

Valerie thought for a moment. "Maybe we don't want her to control it, only summon it," she said tentatively. "Remember when she used it the first time? It sent that giant wave out that not only hurt the Axman but took out every shade in the area. It doesn't seem to hurt normal ghosts so maybe it could be our secret weapon."

"It isn't very secret if everyone knows about it," Shemar pointed out and looked at the younger Maggio. "It could be a boon but if you can't summon it at will, that is a problem. Not to mention that it is unpredictable. It might not have hurt any normal ghosts the first time around, but who's to say it will be that way again? We might as well let the Agency drop the bomb."

"Can we take that off the table, please?" Valerie asked waspishly and the chief threw his hands up. "I still think it would be a benefit for her to at least attempt to get it under control. I don't know how feasible it is since I don't have an empath myself or know how it works, but giving her a way to defend herself wouldn't be a bad idea at this point." She looked pointedly at Marco with her last sentence.

He scratched his head and sighed. "Okay…yeah, I agree with you there."

"Is she comfortable with guns?" Shemar asked. "We could issue her a gun for her protection perhaps."

Annie frowned. "I am…but…"

"But what?"

Macro leaned against the door. "Uh, Chief, maybe I'm wrong, but if the mafia lit his ass up with bullets while he was weak and they didn't end him, he will certainly not flinch at any peashooter you give her."

"Not to mention any of the other times we've fought him and how well the 'shoot first' approach worked. I'm not sure how powerful he is now compared to what he was like at Catherine's house, but it's still enough to worry," Valerie added. "Unless we can sanction her an ether bazooka or something. That might make him lose a step or two."

Shemar clutched the bridge of his nose and mumbled something to himself. "Even if we could, teaching her how to use it properly would probably take about as long as her attempting to learn how to use her empath." He lowered his hands to the desk. "We're already working with the ghost mafia, a witch, and the Agency. I think it is safe to say we're using the kitchen sink approach as it is. She's free to do as she pleases, but when the time comes to face the Axman for real, I don't want her in the fight and certainly not in the front line. But you are right that it might come in handy if she can find a way to control it."

Marco sighed and looked at his sister. "I can try, Annie, but I'll work off of how Pops taught me, and he wasn't exactly some wise sensei or nothing. More like a coach—a kid's baseball coach or something."

"I would think so since that was what he was. He coached both our teams," she pointed out.

"Still, you would have thought this was something you had a fancy teacher for. Then again, maybe he simply didn't want to pay for one." He shrugged and lifted his bat. "Do you have a place where we can get some space?"

Shemar pointed out of the room. "We have converted a small space to a makeshift gym. It's past Simone's office and to the right. Look for the small label on the wall next to the door."

The siblings nodded and Marco opened the door. "All right, Annie, let's give it the old college try."

"You never went to college, Marco," she quipped as they exited.

"Let's hope this goes better, then," he muttered as they left and closed the door behind them.

Valerie watched them go before she sat. "So we have no other options outside of simply hitting him with everything we have?"

Shemar tapped his fingers on the pile of files. "There is the matter of some weapon the mafia are trying to acquire. I don't know what it does but they seem rather pleased about it, which worries me."

"What worries me is that the Axman hasn't appeared yet," she stated and folded her hands together as she worked through her thoughts. "I'm not sure what Aiyana did, but she seems to have bought us some time. You need to call that meeting asap before anyone does something drastic."

As she finished her statement, an uproar outside the office ended the conversation. Both she and Shemar ran out to where officers and civilians looked out of the windows. She pushed past a few of them and scowled at a shimmering light that slowly encased the city. "Chief! What's going on?"

"I don't know," he answered. "I hadn't heard anything about this being authorized."

"Chief!" another officer yelled. "Look at the TV."

They all turned to see Director Lovett on screen. "Citizens of New Orleans. Do not panic. We at the SEA, in collaboration with your government, have begun to erect our proprietary barrier around the city for your protection."

"What the hell?" Valerie growled angrily. "Why now?"

Shemar sighed. "I stalled her with the fact that we didn't have Annie in our protection and we couldn't risk erecting the barrier until we found her. It must have gotten back to her that she had returned."

"This is a massive overreach," she muttered. "The living can still flee, right?"

"Although our barrier only affects ghostly residents, we apologize for the adverse effects you will feel while it is active. We recommend all living citizens to not panic and stay in their homes. The crisis will be over soon. This is merely the first step to eradicate it. You have my promise as co-director that the SEA will end this terror once and for all and you can have your city back."

"Note that she doesn't offer to help rebuild if this goes tits-up," another officer snarked.

The message began to loop and Valerie shook her head and retrieved her phone. "I still have service. I need to text Johnny about this for when he gets back and see if I can make contact with Donovan."

Shemar nodded as he headed to his office. "Do so. I will call a meeting. Let's see if she even shows up."

She nodded as she finished her text, looked out the window at the dome again, and wondered if it would do any good. If the Axman was already in the city, they were trapped in there with him. And what adverse effects was she talking about?

Still, if the Axman was outside the city still, perhaps that gave them a little more time—although she wondered if the barrier could stop him.

CHAPTER EIGHTEEN

In Limbo, a group of ghosts had wandered through a long twisting maze, probably dreamed up by a posse of former artists in life who were bored in eternity. Normally, they weren't the type of sightseers to bother with such a nuisance but they had been given a tip that something enticing was to be found somewhere within. One of them had just stumbled upon it.

"Hey, guys—over here!" he shouted and stared gleefully at a crossing point. "I found our ticket out of here but it doesn't look like it has much juice or whatever left. First come, first served."

"Then it seems I'm lucky to get here first," a deep voice stated. The ghost didn't recognize it and assumed it was probably some drifter who hung out in the area.

He stood to full height and began to turn. "Uh-uh, I don't think so, pal. Me and the boys have been—oh, my God!" He backed away, frightened by the large dark monster who stood behind him. "What the hell have you been eating?"

The Axman chuckled and rested his ax across his shoulder. "Perhaps not eating, exactly, but your friends have given me considerable fuel." Suddenly, he pulled the ax off his shoulder and pointed at the ghost's face. "Now then. I seem to be trapped in this pointless existence like yourself. Where does this portal lead?"

The ghost held his hands up. "I-I don't know, man. H-honest!" he stammered and the lights of his eyes glowed and dimmed erratically. "We were looking for a way outta Limbo and aren't too choosy about it, you know?"

The Axman tilted his head back. "I suppose it doesn't matter for me either. I should be able to return to New Orleans no matter where I end up."

"That sounds great, friend!" The ghost tried to look casually around for an exit. "Take it. I can find another. You seem to be pressed for time and I don't mind strolling around a little longer."

"How kind of you." The Axman lowered his weapon, only to step forward and grasp the ghost by his neck. "Unfortunately, I can't have you strolling around to tell anyone about this little interaction. I have too many distractions as it is."

The hapless victim tried to pry the killer's hands off of him to no avail. The dark phantasma began to slide across the Axman's hand and onto the ghost's face. "Wait, no! I won't tell anyone, I promise you! I promise!" The phantasma covered his face quickly and muffled his words before the body went limp. It turned gray as he lost his green color and his skeletal body began to flake and turn to ash. The Axman turned toward the portal. It did seem frail in comparison to other crossing points he had seen, but he had to agree with the ghost on one point—he could not be too choosy right now.

He walked toward it, left the dark maze, and emerged in a place of blinding white. It took him a moment to adjust but it seemed he was on a mountain top. A storm raged above him and the snow and ice flowed through him while a thick fog surrounded the area. The snow fell in heaps around him and he rather enjoyed the novelty of it. He was quite certain he hadn't seen snow since he was a child so long before.

But he was indeed pressed for time and couldn't linger to reminisce. He lifted his ax and swung it into the ground beneath him. A crevasse opened, a kind of slipstream between the world of the living and the dead that he could use to create crossing points as long as the destination was on the same side.

It was a useful ability—or he'd thought so at first before he had been trapped in Limbo twice now. Still, he'd learned and it would not happen again.

He stepped off the edge, fell into it, and traveled quickly through a flurry of green, black, and white colors to New Orleans. Something was wrong, however. He felt a resistance of some kind as he approached.

Part of him wanted to simply burst through it. After all, what could stop him now? He had the powers of a keeper, albeit a weakened one, but nothing could stop him now, could it? Still, his better judgment prevailed and he ended his trip a tad early. He lurched out and landed in the middle of a street. New Orleans was visible in the distance, along with something unexpected.

Some kind of bubble surrounded the city. It had

certainly not been there before. Intrigued, he floated up and through the sky to land in front of it. He raised a hand and approached it cautiously. The phantasma around his hand begin to shrink and he realized that this was a very concentrated shield of ether.

He lowered to the earth and realized that it must be some kind of Agency device. After a brief study, he identified some kind of machine on the interior of the dome. He walked closer to it but didn't notice the ecto-readers he activated in the process. For a few long moments, he stood in front of the machine—modern technology was not a forte of his—and he could easily assume that this was partially responsible for at least maintaining the blockade.

The Axman swung his ax and drove it into the barrier with all his might. The shield stopped it but it bent and jerked beneath his power. He also noticed that the blade on his ax began to deform as well. It shrank and grew dull, and the dark phantasma on his arm began to shake and thin out to reveal the ghostly skeleton underneath. He grunted and stepped away from the barrier. Immediately, his ax returned to its larger state and the phantasma formed around his arm again.

Both intrigued and irritated, he looked at the dome again. Such a massive amount of ether would not only create a shield but probably seep into the air within. Any supernatural being would feel sickened and weak, a rather devastating effect to those who hadn't felt that way in decades and probably centuries in some cases.

While he could probably simply force it open with his brute strength, he might have to pay a cost. There was no way to know what effect driving himself through it would have on his form and he also didn't even know if it would bring it down entirely or merely create a small hole.

He traced a finger along it. There was something else to it. Ether alone, no matter how strong, wouldn't have this kind of effect on him. It might cause him some pain and minor debilitation, but this felt like it seeped inside him and tried to rip him apart to change him.

A wisp of something familiar floated in the clear energy —something most others probably wouldn't see—and he laughed. It was gray phantasma, barely distinguishable from the ether. He knew where that came from and he had to hand it to those Agency fellas and gals. They were certainly crafty. But, he reminded himself, he was craftier.

The roar of multiple engines caught his attention. He turned to where several large trucks raced toward him. At first, he thought it was merely more fodder for his ax, but he noticed large cannons of some kind on the roofs of the vehicles. They were charging up and aimed directly at him.

He looked at the barrier. They would no doubt pummel him with a similar type of energy. As much as he wanted to show that nothing they had could stand against his might in his present form, the manic side of him was calmed again by the reasonable part of his mind. He swung his ax and drove it into the earth as the cannons fired.

A large blast of white bloomed in the area where the Axman had stood. The vehicles came to a stop. The sides of a couple opened and several agents leapt out and aimed at the spot with their rifles and personal cannons. "Do we have confirmation on a hit?" one asked.

"I don't see anything," another announced and shrugged. "But the shots were dead on."

"Yeah, well, I've heard this guy can take a hell of a beating," the former responded. "Make sure to stay on your toes and we'll be back at HQ by mid—"

One of the vehicles flipped when the Axman bounded out of a crevasse below it. Before they could even turn, three were cut down with one blow. The three other trucks turned their cannons quickly toward him to fire, but he rushed at the closest one and barreled into its side. It flipped and landed on top of another that began to slide toward the next.

That truck drove hastily out of the way, but the change in direction caused the cannon's shot to miss and fly over the Axman's head. The phantasma on his head peeled away to reveal his skeletal features.

"He's exposed!" one shouted and aimed her rifle. "Shoot him now!" She fired, but a split second before the shot struck, the phantasma coated him again and he snatched her by the front of her jacket.

"That wouldn't have worked even if the shot had landed." He sneered and crushed his giant hand around her chest. "As your friend said, I can take a beating. Let's see how good you are at it." He flung her at the other vehicle, which tried to aim its cannon at him again. She pounded into the windshield and her body began to slide down. The driver was distracted and didn't see a giant ax crash through the window and through him as well.

The Axman felt pinpricks and small blasts of cold around his body. He turned to the remaining agents, who attempted to fell him with their weapons. If he weren't so annoyed, he might have applauded their bravado. He raised his hand and his ax returned to him. One of the agents ran up and lobbed some kind of explosive at him, but he batted it away and it erupted behind him. He rushed at the remaining agents and slaughtered them all. Ten agents were dead with three swings of his ax.

The Axman didn't take a moment to gloat or revel since he knew that was probably only the first wave and he had more pressing concerns. He closed his eyes. While he might have been trapped outside the barrier, his shades were not. He reached out to where they flew mindlessly inside.

A few dozen remained, but being under the assault of the barrier's ether made them drop like flies. He quickly took control of them and gave them a simple command to find the source of the barrier. His mind sensed them all fan out. At first, they searched buildings and the street but he knew it wouldn't be that obvious.

He looked at the machine and when he noticed the cords below, he brought one of the shades to it and instructed it to follow them. They led to a generator but it wasn't what he was looking for. Perhaps if he destroyed it, the barrier would weaken, but he now had other plans.

A blast blew his shade apart without warning. The Axman was momentarily blind before he punched the dome out of anger and immediately clutched his hand when the phantasma melted off. He quickly took control of another and directed it to where the first had been destroyed. It floated carefully in shadowed areas to make sure it wasn't seen easily.

A group of agents and a truck loitered in front of a nondescript red brick building and their presence immediately aroused his curiosity. He had the shade phase into the building and when an alarm blared, he at least knew something important was there.

With roughly thirty shades left, he needed to move fast. He summoned the others to the building as he made his shade dash madly through the building to the basement. It housed a large device with a cylindrical base and a large bowl-like attachment that pointed up. This was surrounded by ether, but what was alongside it was more important. A compartment held the remnants of a wraith.

Also in that room was a large number of agents who all fired at the shade. He released it and switched to another, this one among a mass of others that flew into the building and ignored the guards outside. He made them all immediately attack the basement. When the mass distracted the guards, he made his fly to the device. It began to dissipate as it drew closer but it managed to break the tank and yank out the container holding the wraith essence.

The Axman returned his focus to himself and heard more vehicles approaching. Quickly, he bulldozed into the ether barrier, which bent much more easily. Although he could feel the cold of the ether fighting against him, it could no longer stop him. He was able to break apart enough of the barrier to slip through and stepped inside before he created another crevasse and used it to slip into the Agency's makeshift lab.

When he appeared, only ten or so of his minions were left but all the agents immediately turned their attention to trying to fight their main target. This allowed the shades a chance to knock over or strike down the various agents and lab techs while the Axman approached the machine.

He pushed easily through the smaller ether barrier

around it, picked the container up, and let his dark phantasma flow into it and combine with the wraith essence. It dominated it, then destroyed it, and only his phantasma remained. He placed it into the machine and turned as more agents entered the basement, only to be bowled over by the remaining shades.

The Axman simply stepped on or over them as he ascended the stairs and left the building. When he looked up, web-like tendrils of dark phantasma began to coat the sky.

They had been running for so long. He had fought those damn nuisances for too long. With this, he would control the city. Then he would bring the whole life and death nonsense to an end and he would never have to worry about what awaited him beyond since he wouldn't have to return to it.

But before that, he needed to prepare. His two main domains were compromised now and it would take him a while to prepare a new chamber with all the proper sigils.

Well, except for one.

CHAPTER NINETEEN

Vic returned slowly to his senses in a room he didn't remember and looked around at a couple of beds, a TV, and some paintings that looked like trees or something. They told him he was probably in a hotel room but he wasn't sure how he got there.

He stood up and dusted himself off, not that it did anything. The last thing he remembered was being on the roof with the huntsmen and Samedi. He'd seen a glow or something and began to feel sick. God, he hadn't felt that awful in decades—since that bachelor party in '68 back when he was alive. He'd thought one of the few real pros to the whole ghost situation was never having to feel like that again.

His head cleared somewhat and he looked around the room again. He must have phased through the building while he dealt with whatever the hell that was. It had felt like ether but different. He glanced out the window and noticed it was getting dark, which made him wonder how long he'd been out.

Something was missing, though. He frowned as he explored the feeling. Some*one* was missing—shit, Johnny! Vic attempted to float and discovered that he was slower than he was accustomed to. His phasing wasn't particularly great either and he was almost stuck between floors while he ascended. When he finally reached the rooftop, Johnny sat with his head in his hands while Samedi looked down at him.

"Hey, kid!" Vic shouted as he pulled himself onto the roof and walked closer. "Are you feeling all right?"

It looked like his partner wanted to nod but his head merely leaned to the left. "I feel like I'm gonna vomit," he admitted ruefully. "What happened?"

"I'm not sure. That dome went up and I started to feel like I ingested poison. Trust me, I'm speaking from experience." He helped the young detective to his feet. "I guess you got some effects too given the bond and all. Sorry about that. There are pros and cons to everything." He patted Samedi on the chest. "Thanks for looking after him for me, Baron." No reply came from the loa, who stared at the sky. "Samedi?"

The keeper looked grimly at the ghost detective. "I am happy you are well now, but it appears we may not wish to celebrate quite yet." He pointed up. "If anything, this is not much of an improvement."

Alarmed, the partners looked up to where dark patches obscured the sky and expanded slowly around the entire dome. "What is that?" Johnny gasped.

"Ah, hell." Vic growled in annoyance. "That looks like the Axman's junky phantasma."

"He is here," Kaitō declared.

The ghost detective nodded. "Yeah, that's probably a safe bet."

"Get back!" the huntsman warned and drew his sword. They followed his gaze and instantly drew their guns as the Axman approached them. Kaitō beat them to it and sliced through his neck before he spun and cut the remains of his body vertically in half. They all stared as the pieces disappeared and the hunter looked confused. "That was the monster you have feared all this time?"

Vic lowered his weapon and shook his head. "I wish. We would have closed this case by now."

"That was only a clone—basically a modified shade or something," the revenant explained and holstered his weapon. "I guess he's back at it but I kind of wish he had more tricks."

Screams erupted below. "Kaitō, more terrors have appeared!" one of the other huntsmen called.

The group hurried to the edge and peered over. Below, shades, shadows, and Axman clones seemingly attacked everything from bystanders to random items such as door fronts and streetlights.

"Either the Axman has lost it or he's trying to make a statement," Vic muttered.

The samurai held his blade up. "My brothers, we have more to do. To arms!" he cried as he leapt off the building along with his comrades.

"Wait!" Johnny cried but if they heard him, they did not comply. He slammed a fist on the edge of the roof and sighed as he dug through his pockets. "We could have used them. This is only a distraction." He finally found his phone and took it out. "I need to call Valerie and see—oh, she texted me." He opened the text. "They have Annie and are at the precinct."

"Again?" The ghost detective snorted. "The Axman will probably head straight there at some point. To get rid of an annoyance if nothing else. She'd be better hiding in a crack house." He shook his head and turned to Samedi. "Baron, are you with us?"

The loa straightened. "I did not come here to sightsee. Do you have a plan?"

"I have a defensive tactic." He pointed to the west. "Can you take us to the police precinct?"

"Are we going to recover the girl?"

"We're going to guard her for now," he stated. "As much as the police precinct might be predictable, I guess it is one of the few places that can be defended without turning to the Agency or mafia for protection. The Axman may be powerful again but I doubt he wants to confront you directly right now. If he shows up and sees you, it might make him think twice about trying to bullrush his way to Annie."

"Ah, so I am to be a bodyguard," the loa commented with a shrug. "That is certainly within my role. Fuse, you two."

"Fuse?" Johnny asked in bewilderment but Vic simply nodded and phased into him. "Why do we need to—hey!" Samedi picked him up by the back of his jacket and floated skyward before he streaked over the city to the police precinct. They landed and the young man flailed to maintain his balance. "Couldn't you have simply made a portal or something?"

Samedi nodded as he took a few steps forward. "I could

have but I'm trying to conserve my power. It's not as easy on the living side and I did just close a tear between worlds, remember?"

"What the hell? Freeze!" a cop shouted and looked straight at the baron as he drew his sidearm. Several others gasped and did the same as Samedi held his arms up lack-adaisically.

"Quite the welcome," he quipped as Vic revealed himself quickly.

"You might want to put those down guys!" he yelled. "For three reasons. He's here to help, shooting him won't do nothing anyway, and there is a good chance he'll decide your fate when you die—which could be real soon if we don't get this situation resolved real quick, all right?"

"What's going on?" Shemar demanded as he walked out of the precinct and halted only a few steps down the stairs when he saw Samedi. "Who the—man, I see strange things all the time but not so many at once." He sighed.

Valerie came out after him and saw the two detectives. "Johnny, Vic!" she shouted, rushed down the steps, and tried to get the other officers to lower their weapons. "It's all right. They are helping with the case."

"And how's that been going so far?" one of the officers asked snidely.

She ignored him and approached quickly when she noticed the keeper beside them. "Baron Samedi?"

"Ah, Valerie, it feels like so long ago that we first met." The loa greeted her with a small bow. "I suppose that's what the living mean by a 'long day,' hmm?"

"He's come to help, Val," Vic told her as he floated

closer. "We took care of Kriminel but the Axman got the last of his juice."

"We noticed," she remarked and pointed at the sky. "It's some kind of contamination of the central whatever grid of the Agency's shield. The Axman tampered with it somehow and now, he's running things. They are trying to get control of it again but the place is crawling with all his little minions."

"They're also marching through the streets," Johnny added and noticed Shemar ordering the other officers to lower their weapons. "Maybe not literally, but they are tearing everything up fairly indiscriminately."

Vic beckoned to Samedi. "We assumed that he'll head this way eventually. Samedi has offered to watch over Annie until we decide how we can bring the fight to him."

"Where is she now?" the revenant asked.

Valerie looked at Samedi and then at the precinct building. "She's in there with her brother. They are trying to find a way to tap into her empath."

Samedi made an affirmative clicking sound. "Is that so? It's always fun to watch a new empath grow into their powers." He began to float away toward the building. "Perhaps I can provide a pointer or two."

The other officers watched in awe as the giant keeper moved past. Shemar merely gave him a curt nod as he approached the group. "Our building is starting to look like an exhibit."

"It's better than a mausoleum," Vic countered and scowled at the barrier. "Who's bright idea was this?"

"Director Lovett and the mayor, I believe." The chief grimaced.

"Any news on the dome?" Johnny asked. "Can people get out?"

Valerie shook her head. "We only got early reports but the teams that are investigating it say they can't cross. A couple of poor bastards touched the stuff and croaked before they even had time to fall over. The dome was only supposed to lock ghosts in but it seems both living and dead alike are stuck in here."

Shemar sighed in exasperation and focused on Vic. "Please tell me you have some better news."

"Only that Kriminel is dead," the ghost detective stated and scratched the back of his head under his hat. "I suppose the only other thing I can offer is a reasonable deduction."

"Good or bad?"

"It depends on how you look at it." He cleared his throat as he folded his arms. "But we're in the endgame now. The Axman has this place locked down and is on a second warpath. And like any sequel, it's bigger and worse than the first. We got what we got and we'll have to make do."

Shemar and Valerie exchanged looks. "It's easy to see how that's bad," he responded. "What's good about it exactly?"

The ghost detective tilted his head. "It means this will probably be over, one way or another, in a few hours." He stared Shemar dead in his eyes. "How that ends for us all depends on what we do between now and then."

The police chief held his head as he came to terms with the fact that he had to agree with him. "I'm open to suggestions if you have any."

Vic rubbed his chin in thought. "Well, we have to find

him first—assuming he doesn't come to us. But my guess is he'll get impatient soon enough. I'm sure he realizes as much as we do that the end is near. On top of that, he's probably gotten big in the head since he took Kriminel's essence, so he'll possibly be sloppy."

"Does he need to worry about anything with that kind of power?" Valerie asked.

He looked at her. "You've already seen what he's like when he thinks he's king big dick. He's prone to boasting and likes to make a scene. That keeps him around and this time, we got a keeper to back us up."

"Do you honestly think we can do this?" Shemar asked.

The ghost detective tilted his hat and nodded. "When the mook starts getting desperate, you know that you're starting to get him right where you want him. I ain't saying this will end neatly, but I think we have our shot ready and lined up."

"Incoming!" an officer shouted. They looked up as several shades streaked from the sky, but several quick shots eliminated them before they even had a chance to reach the street.

Everyone looked at Johnny, who lowered his gun calmly and shrugged. "I've had practice over the last couple of days," he explained.

"I doubt that'll be the only things headed our way," Shemar noted, pointed to a group of officers, and sent them up the street. "I need to get back inside to coordinate everything. We'll go over our final plan shortly. Until then, do what you can."

"Of course," Vic said with a nod. "We'll be ready."

The police chief nodded and they shook hands as he

turned and left. Johnny holstered his weapon as he walked closer. "You know, I never took you for a moody guy, Vic, but I also never took you for such an optimist."

The ghost slid his hands into his jacket pockets. "Eh, there's enough doom and gloom around. Offering some hope, even if it's only a touch, will do wonders right now." He looked at Valerie. "Hey, Val. How are you holding up?"

The officer shrugged. "We got Annie back but we lost Aiyana."

"What?" The revenant gasped and Vic's lights dimmed.

"She sacrificed herself so we could get Annie out. I don't know what she did but she bought us the time we needed and the Axman hasn't come for us since we got back."

"Hmm," Vic muttered. "When Kriminel was about to die, he was somehow connected to the Axman, albeit briefly. Aiyana may have tried to trap him in Limbo."

Johnny shook himself out of his stupor. "It was probably the only way she thought she could truly stop him. It didn't seem to take, though."

"No, but it gives me an idea," the ghost said quickly. "He didn't immediately follow us either when he tried to nab Annie that time in the store parking lot. He was able to send himself into Limbo, but it seems he has trouble getting out." He began to whisper something to himself, vocalizing his thoughts as he tried to work through them. "I see some possibilities but until we get a bead on him, they'll have to wait."

"Are we going to go find him?" Johnny asked.

He nodded. "The car should still be in the parking lot, right?"

"Are you guys going after him alone?" Valerie asked, wide-eyed. "Are you crazy?"

"Eh, kinda." The revenant grinned. "We wouldn't be here in the first place if we weren't."

"We're only going to look for him," Vic clarified. "Neither one of us is exactly the carpe diem type. We'll make sure everyone knows where he is when the time comes. If you can, make sure everyone is ready to go once we do."

"Are you that confident that you can find him?" she asked.

Johnny shrugged. "It's kind of what we do." He looked at his partner. "Although I'm interested to hear where you think we should start because I draw a blank."

"I have an idea." Vic placed a hand on Valerie's shoulder. "Are you gonna be all right?"

She nodded. "I have a shit-ton to worry about for now so I'll keep busy. Shemar was trying to call a meeting with all the parties before you arrived. I need to see if we can at least get the mafia here to talk as the Agency has seemingly decided to do their own thing." She looked briefly at the barrier in annoyance. "A fat lot of good that did. Maybe they'll show a little humility now. Wait a minute—Donovan!" She yanked her phone out. "He went to recover something out at sea hours ago. I wonder if he made it back."

"Hopefully, it was something worth it." Johnny huffed.

"You guys go. I need to make a call," she told them. The partners nodded and headed to the parking lot as she pressed the agent's number. The phone rang three times with no reply and didn't even give her a chance to leave a message. "Dammit, Donovan, where are you?"

CHAPTER TWENTY

"It's one damn thing after another, huh?" Rick muttered as they pulled into port. He looked at the dark webbing in the sky and then at Donovan. "Are you telling me this was your ace in the hole?"

"Don't look at me." The agent sighed and folded his arms. "I was with you this entire time. I wasn't made aware that they intended to activate the barrier." He scowled at the swirling black spots. "And it sure as hell shouldn't look like that."

"You know, if we were only a couple of minutes late, we wouldn't have gotten in. Then again, I felt like I was gonna puke once we were inside until that gunk started to fill the sky." The mobster rolled his eyes. "Great lines of communication you have in the SEA," he mocked and leaned out to see the pier coming into view. "I, on the other hand, can tell you that the don will be waiting for us once we arrive. He was quite pleased to learn that we succeeded."

"You've been a part of the New Orleans chapter for the

most part, right?" Donovan asked. "Have you seen the don in person much?"

"Eh, here and there. He's fairly high strung but he's also run the entire ghost mob for more than half a century. I'd probably get that way too after only a few years." He beckoned one of his soldiers. "Hey, Jimmy, go grab a few of the others and make sure the cannon is ready when we disembark."

"Sure thing, Rick, but…uh, we're kinda running low on stygia," the mobster admitted.

"Are you kidding me? There's a boatload of the stuff in those crates. Break one open and pass it around to anyone who needs it, but make sure everything is ready. Come on, now—chop-chop!" he ordered. Jimmy nodded and ran off, enlisted a couple of others, and hurried into the cargo hold.

"You certainly have the loyalty of your men," Donovan noted. "Are you expecting a promotion after all this is said and done?"

Rick tilted his head. "Maybe, if we all get out of this intact. I assume there will be all kinds of shuffling once this is over." He was silent for a moment. "You've made a career out of hunting guys like this Axman asshole. Tell me, what do you honestly think our chances are?"

The agent straightened and regarded him calmly. "I have to say this is probably the most perilous case I've had during my tenure in the Agency, but believe it or not, it is far from the worst situation I've heard about."

"Seriously?" The mobster's snort became a rough laugh. "That's somehow both comforting and terrifying. So you think we got a shot?"

"Of course I do," he replied and raised an eyebrow at his companion. "Are you telling me you've done all this and you don't think so?"

Rick shrugged and removed his hands from the railing. "To tell you the truth, I've been doing this because I wanted to make sure that if this was it, I went down fighting rather than waiting for this *Verme* to hack my head off and send me away to nothingness." He rolled his shoulders and sighed. "You know, it's a pity you aren't a ghost. I saw some top-shelf stygian wine and cigars in a couple of those crates down there."

"Is that so?"

"Yeah. Once this is all over, I'll want to celebrate." He chuckled. "I probably got some real cash stashed in a sock or something somewhere. I'll get you something more palatable to salute with."

Donovan nodded. "I will certainly be in the mood for it. You know, the Agency does have some experimental tonics they've been working on. Most were deemed failures because they seemed to get the ghosts drunker than anything else."

"For real?"

The agent nodded. "Yeah. Okay, others caused things like holes to appear on the bodies or their color to change, but I think I remember which one is which."

The mobster shook his head with a grin. "I think I'll stick with the normal stuff, buddy."

"We're coming into port!" Bobby announced over the intercom. "It looks like we got some friends awaiting us."

Rick, Donovan, and a handful of agents and mobsters walked to the port side of the ship. When the bridge lowered, Don Pesci and several other mobsters awaited them. "It's about time you got back." He groaned as they approached and pointed at the agent. "Hey, what the hell is with this thing over the city?"

Donovan leaned against the ropes. "It is supposed to be a protective barrier against supernatural beings." He looked up slightly. "Compromised, by the looks of it."

"That's it?" the mob boss demanded.

"That's all I know—and I'm guessing about the latter part. I wasn't aware that they were even activating it."

"I can vouch for him, sir," Rick added. "He seemed as bamboozled as we were."

Pesci looked at him and took a drag of his cigar "Fine. We have other things to worry about. So what happened?"

"Some terrors invaded the ship," he replied. "We took care of them and secured the shipment. I got some of my boys bringing the package up and everything else is accounted for."

The don nodded and took a long look at the ship. "Any survivors?"

"Outside of us? No, sir."

He shook his head. "Dammit. I'm gonna be buying a shitload of flowers after this is all said and done." He perked up when several mafiosos carried a large crate onto the pier. "Is this it?"

"Yes, sir." Rick floated to the crate and motioned for his men to open it. "I had a chance to...ah, see it in operation." They removed the lid and Pesci and a few of his men peered inside. "It certainly lives up to expectations."

"I wish you got it on video or something," the mob boss muttered. "We need to see if this will be enough to obliterate the Axman the next time we have him in our crosshairs."

"Don!" one of the mobsters shouted in a panic. "Don—we got intruders!"

Everyone spun as a mass of shades and shadows appeared at the port. "What the hell?" Pesci yelled as everyone with a weapon began to either shoot, stab, or bludgeon the terrors. Their numbers seemed to grow by the second, although many began to fall to the onslaught. Amongst them, a large figure appeared. He stood frozen and stared down the dock at the don. "Is that..." Pesci muttered and pointed at the new arrival. "That's Axman—it's the Axman!" He turned to Rick. "Don't just stand there. Bring the cannon out!"

The Axman began to charge toward them. Mobsters tried to gun him down or get in his way but fell to brutal slashes from his ax. Rick and several of his men began to get the cannon out of the box while Donovan and his agents joined the fight. However, while their adversary approached, the agent looked at the mobsters as they tried to prepare the cannon and noticed that one tried to take out a large cylinder of ether that made his hands crumble.

"Anderson, with me!" he ordered. The sharpshooter took one final shot at a shadow and nodded when it disappeared. The two ran to the cannon. Donovan took the front as he asked Rick, "What do we need to do?"

"It needs to be reloaded," the mobster answered and slid a large compartment at the back of the cannon open. "Pull the old one out and slide the new one in." Anderson grasped the handle of the old charge, twisted it, and hauled it out. She let it fall as she took the new one and placed it inside, then slid the compartment shut. Donovan rested the front on his shoulder and held the trigger down to let it charge. "Everyone needs to get out of the way!"

"Don!" Rick shouted as Pesci held his shotgun up and blasted a nearby shade into the water. "Everyone needs to move! This ain't no joke!"

The don nodded and fired his shotgun into the air. "Move it or lose your bones!" he ordered as he and his men floated off to the sides of the pier. "This won't play favorites, nimrods!"

By this point, the Axman was almost halfway down the pier. The mob boss and his men maintained a steady barrage of shots at him but if he was bothered by any of it, he didn't show it. "Steady, Anderson," the agent called as he positioned their adversary dead in the sights. "Firing in three!"

"To hell with that—fire now!" Rick shouted as he floated off to the side. The agent didn't retort and simply agreed as he loosed the trigger and the blast of the cannon knocked him and his subordinate back and almost into the water. The orb of ether and who knew what sailed across the wooden walkway and pounded into the Axman. His eyes lit and the blast echoed across the pier. The mobsters saw the wave coming and even the heartiest and sternest soldiers scrambled out of the way as shades and shadows alike erupted into nothingness the second the blast caught them. Pesci watched with such awe that two of his men had to grab him and pull him back from the arc of the wave to make sure he wouldn't be hit by it.

Donovan got to his knees and scowled as the Axman

withered and turned briefly into a shadow before he disappeared. He slammed a fist on the dock. "Dammit!"

"What's the matter?" Rick asked when he floated to his side as the energy diminished. "That was it, wasn't it? We won!"

The agent pushed to his feet and shook his head. "No, we didn't. That was only a clone."

"A clone?" Pesci screeched as he returned to the pier. "We wasted a shot on some doppelganger?"

Anderson placed her end of the cannon down carefully and walked to the crate. "If each shot requires one of these tubes for ammo, we only have one shot left unless there's more on board."

Donovan looked at Rick for his reply, who in turn looked at the don. "Uh...well, I didn't see anymore. I'm still getting a count of everything in the hold but—"

"We got nothing," Pesci said with an exasperated sigh. "It's still new tech and the guys we bought it from ain't exactly making it themselves. We got all we could from them so it means we have one shot left."

He turned to one of his guards. "Bring the cars and trucks around and let's get them loaded." The ghost nodded and left quickly as the don turned to the group. "We got that last shot so let's be sure we make it count, all right? But we got all the other weapons to hand out to anyone who can hold them." He took another cigar out. "The police chief has been trying to hold another meeting. We might as well attend and see where we stand." He regarded Donovan with a raised eyebrow as he snipped the end of his cigar and one of his guards offered him a lighter. "Do you think your boss will show up?"

The agent shrugged. He could call her, of course, but given how things had gone, he wondered if that would do more harm than good. Lovett was too strict with protocol and given how well the barrier had worked out, she didn't seem like the right person to call at the moment. "I don't know. But the mission for me and my team is to take care of the Axman by any means necessary so you have us at least."

Pesci took a drag. "That's fine by me. You seem more agreeable anyway." The vehicles began to load up at the end of the docks and the don made a circle in the air. "All right, everyone. I want those trucks to be spilling with goods." He pointed to Rick and Donovan. "You two bring some guys with you. You're with me."

"No problem, boss." The mafioso nodded and gestured to Sam, Jake, and Jimmy.

Anderson tapped Donovan on the shoulder. "Are you sure about this, sir? There will more than likely be repercussions for this."

He folded his rifle and placed it on his back. "You are probably right, but it could be the end of life as we know it. I'll worry about that tomorrow." He held a hand out. "Are you with me?"

Anderson looked at it as the rest of his team approached. She looked back as they all stood ready before she nodded and shook it. "Always, sir."

CHAPTER TWENTY-ONE

"Concentrate," Marco said as Annie held the bat out in front of her as if it were a samurai sword. "You gotta...uh, you know—feel it."

"Feel it?" she asked exasperatedly as she let the bat hang in her hands. "What does that even mean, Marco?"

Her brother shrugged. "I'm not too sure myself. I'm parroting whatever Dad told me."

"Well, something had to click." She took the bat in both hands and swung it idly. "What finally got it to work for you?"

He leaned against the wall. "Working on it for a long time. I had no problem activating it, only maintaining it. But it took me a few years. I wasn't like I used it for anything but chasing out the ghost riff-raff from time to time." He looked at the bat in her hands. "We don't even know if it's the same thing. My color is blue, yours is white, and mine sure as hell doesn't go off like an atom bomb."

"And that would be very useful right now." Annie sighed and dropped the bat on the floor. She pulled a folding chair out and slumped on it. "He's coming again eventually, Marco."

Her brother pushed off the wall and walked over to comfort her. "Yeah, but he won't take you again. Everyone is preparing to take him down now. You don't have to be scared, Annie."

"I want to help, though," she protested and looked into his eyes. "I don't want to cower in a basement again. I've had to do that since we were dragged into this. I have the ability to help but it's simply not working!"

"Perhaps I can be of some assistance?" The siblings turned to a large ghost with tribal markings and glowing purple eyes who looked down at them. "I would also think you would like a little payback as well."

Marco lunged quickly for the bat. "Who the hell are you?"

"Marco!" Annie shouted and stopped him from wielding it. "It's all right. This is Baron Samedi—he's a keeper. He was the one who sent Johnny and Vic on the case."

"I nudged them," Samedi admitted and shrank slightly so he didn't tower over the siblings. "It is good to see you safe, Annie. I also heard about the loss that came with it and for that, I am sorry."

Annie nodded and lowered her head. "Aiyana, yes." She took the bat from Marco and held it gingerly in her hands. "That's why I want to fight as well—for everyone the Axman has hurt and for all the sacrifices that happened because of me."

Samedi cocked his head and placed a hand on her shoulders. "Do not think that way, child. You have had to shoulder a terrible burden because of the Axman and my brother's madness. Their wrongs should not chain you now." He lifted her head so they looked at one another. "But I understand your sentiment and I believe you could be a great asset in the fight to come."

She looked at the bat again. "I think so too but I don't know how I got my empath to work the first time." She looked at Marco. "I saw the Axman attempt to kill my brother and it simply happened."

"There are numerous ways for an empath to manifest," the baron stated, took the bat, and examined it. "I take it your brother needs this as a focus?"

Marco nodded. "Yeah. Any bat will do as long as it's wood. It's something to do with a familiar connection or something."

"I see." He handed it back to him. "Perhaps that is necessary for you but it may not be for her."

"What do you mean?" she asked.

Samedi placed his hands together. "When using an empath ability, you channel phantasma—the very essence of ghosts. The way it reacts varies, but it is better to think of it as magic. I assume you've read stories about such things?" When she nodded, he continued. "You may think you need a bat because your ability used your brother's like a conduit, but that is merely what you are familiar with. It can be a little complicated and in situations like these, it is better to learn from a more knowledgeable figure."

"I knew I should have told Pops not to cheap out," Marco muttered.

The loa clicked his tongue a few times in thought. "Bring your hands together—like so." He placed his palms together and Annie followed his lead. "This is only practice, but I would like you to attempt to summon the phantasma to you."

She looked at her hands. "Summon it to me? I don't know where to begin."

"That is all right. Phantasma exists in both the realm of the living and the dead. If you are an empath, it gravitates naturally to you. Consider this an experiment if you will." He opened his palms. "Close your eyes and think back to that moment when it came to you but don't think of the anger or the fear. Instead, think of wanting to protect your brother and defend him against the Axman."

Annie closed her eyes and thought back to the fight. A chill ran through her but she continued the memory to when she attacked the Axman with only a bat. It had been a foolish thing to do but she couldn't let her brother die. That was the strongest feeling of all. In a way, it was a prayer she sent out to anyone or anything that would listen and in that moment, something answered.

"Whoa." Marco gasped. "Annie, look!"

She opened her eyes slightly. A pure white orb rested in her hands with what appeared to be flames dancing atop it. "This is…what is this?" she asked and marveled at it. "It reminds me of Aiyana's flames."

Samedi leaned down to study it. "This is something quite pure, my friends." His hands danced above it. "Something I have not seen in a long while now. As you've probably seen with terrors, phantasma can be corrupted and misshapen into something dark and evil but it works in the opposite way as well." He grasped the orb gently on both sides and lifted it. "But to see phantasma of such purity is something most rare. The fact that you are able to summon it in the world of the living is spectacular. I would think that in Limbo, it could be even greater."

"Aiyana told me that her spirits granted her many of her abilities," Annie recalled and stared at her hands when she noticed traces of white phantasma lining her palms. "Is this the same?"

The baron placed the orb into her hands. "Maybe. It's certainly not something I have seen from other empaths and I've seen a lot in my time." He tilted his head and continued to examine the orb. "If it is a gift, it is certainly from someone quite special."

"So you aren't the only one looking after my sister?" Marco asked. "Do you have any idea who it might be?"

He considered it but before he could answer, they heard gunshots from outside. Distracted, Annie dropped the orb and it disappeared before it touched the floor. "Oh no!"

"Calm yourself, child. It is not truly gone," Samedi assured her. The gunshots grew louder. "Although it seems we have little time to continue this lesson. We should probably see what is creating this ruckus."

"This is Officer Simone. We are under attack!" Valerie snapped into her radio as she fired into a swarm of shadows that approached the station. "If anyone near the station is available, we could use backup."

"I'm afraid this might be it," another officer informed her as he fired his rifle. "Everyone is spread throughout the city and probably facing more of these."

"Then we'll have to hold them here until the last one is dropped," she replied.

"I can help with that," Samedi told her from where he floated overhead.

"Val!" Marco called as he and Annie raced up to her. "Are you all right?"

The officer nodded but aimed her gun quickly as a group of shades descended upon them. "Look out!"

The loa didn't even look back. He merely swung an arm that collided with one of the shades. A flash of purple light erupted and the entire group disappeared. "The Axman's minions are no bother to me," he growled and raised his other arm toward the coming onslaught of shadows. "But they are a nuisance."

Tendrils of purple phantasma launched to skewer all the shadows and pulled them to him before they encircled downed officers and civilians. Samedi closed his fist and the shadows were yanked apart. They turned into blasts of dark phantasma that fell earthward before they disappeared.

"Wow." Valerie looked admiringly at the keeper. "Thanks."

"Did I miss anything?" The group looked at Castecka, who brushed her ethereal hair. "It got awful noisy out here." She looked up as Samedi descended. "Oh, my word!"

The loa looked at her in amusement. "A witch? And who's side are you on?"

"The right one," she replied and stepped back. "Whichever you deem that to be."

Valerie stepped between them. "She's all right, Baron. She helped us free Annie."

The keeper's eyebrows raised. "Did she? A helpful witch, is it? You seem to be a rare breed." He looked around the group and chuckled. "I must admit, we have gathered a rather unique group here, haven't we?"

"You're telling me," another voice agreed, followed by the flick of a lighter.

"Marsan." Samedi greeted him cheerfully. "Good of you to join us."

"Where the hell have you been?" Valerie chided.

Big Daddy closed his lighter and took a drag of his cigar. "I went to drop Cathy off with some of my friends who could take care of her. It was fairly obvious that this wasn't exactly the safest place right now." He looked at the loa. "I saw the tear was closed. How are you holding up, Baron?"

Samedi held his hands casually behind his back as he looked at the remnants on the street. "I must admit, I am weaker after everything than I thought. Normally, I should be able to take care of paltry things like that with a look." He sighed and scratched his head. "I should save myself for the main event as it were."

"Look out— dybbuk!" an officer shouted. They all looked at the hooded horror that hovered menacingly above them. The keeper held a hand up but before he could do anything, a sword thrust through its head and it fell apart. A ghost in samurai armor appeared behind it.

"Kaitō." The loa clapped as he descended. "Very well-timed."

The huntsman sheathed his blade. "I've been looking for you, Keeper."

He shrugged in response. "As I recall, you were the one who ran off."

"I went to hunt," he corrected. "And what have you done, loa? Are you any closer to finding the Axman?"

"Is there not enough prey for you, huntsman?" The baron scoffed.

"We are not here for pleasure," Kaitō retorted. "We are here to send the Axman into oblivion or return him to Hell. Once that is done, the living can fend for themselves from here on."

"Thank God you won't stick around," Valerie whispered.

"Cars on approach," an officer stated. They all turned to where a caravan of three cars pulled up.

One of the doors opened, and the first to step out were agents in full gear. Valerie prepared to give them an earful when mafia ghosts also began to fan out. One of the agents approached her and removed his helmet to reveal a familiar face. "It's good to see you in one piece, Officer."

"Donovan," she replied, both relieved and perplexed. "I guess it is nice to see you too. Assuming you are still on our side."

He nodded. "To be fair, the Agency certainly isn't on the Axman's side but I know what you mean."

"Hello, Agent," Shemar said as he joined the group.

"Chief Shemar." He nodded a greeting. "I heard you called a meeting. Is the director here?"

"No, and I don't think she'll come. I haven't been able to make contact with her since the barrier went up," the police chief stated. "In this situation, you are here and still seem like you want to kick ass instead of wanting to run the show. So if you are with us, I'll certainly take the help."

Donovan nodded and gestured behind him with his thumb. "Of course, but I should also point out that I'm with him as well." They all looked to where Don Pesci approached.

The mob boss looked around the group with interest. "Mafia, cops, agents, and now the Wild Hunt and...a keeper?"

Samedi almost seemed offended. "Do you honestly not remember me, Robert? I was one of the few keepers willing to listen to your bargain." He poked the don with a large finger. "You still owe me for that fancy suit and title you're wearing."

The don grimaced and adjusted his jacket. "Are you here to collect? Now isn't exactly a good time, you know."

"Help us finish this mess and I'd say we're even."

"Done. That was the plan anyway," Pesci finished with a nod. He clapped and rubbed his hands together. "Now, what are we doing about this mess? I got a load of guns and a special present for that bastard once I get my hands on him again."

"For now, we're trying to find him," Shemar admitted. "We have two guys looking into it, but the city still needs help. I'm sending as many men and women out as I can but those damn things keep attacking the station. I have a feeling he may show up anytime now."

"I think he may be lying in wait," Kaitō countered. "He is growing more powerful and his terrors more plentiful. He's merely waiting for the right moment to strike once we're overwhelmed."

"Then we shouldn't sit here twiddling our thumbs!" Pesci shouted and pointed to the police chief. "You said you got two guys looking for him? Where they at?"

Shemar looked at Valerie. "Have you heard anything from them yet?"

She checked her phone and shook her head. "No, but Vic said his hunch was a fair distance away so they might be a while."

"Did they tell you where they were going?" Big Daddy asked.

"No, but they left in a hurry." She looked down the street in the direction in which they had gone. "I only hope they find him and don't jump the gun once they do."

CHAPTER TWENTY-TWO

Johnny tried to close the car door as quietly as possible just in case. "Do you honestly think he might have come here? We already checked this place."

"I'm going by instinct," Vic replied and looked at the factory. "The witch's hut is outside the barrier and the theater is burned down. He might have other hiding places but this is one we know about."

The revenant began to walk around the car but saw something behind the trees. He approached it as his partner moved closer to the entrance. "Vic!" he called quietly. "I think we may have a lead here."

"What?" The ghost's eyes dimmed when he saw what Johnny was talking about. "Oh."

The corpses of five agents sprawled together, all with slash marks. The young detective knelt and examined them. "We don't have a field kit but I think it is safe to say that all these wounds look like they were inflicted by a large bladed weapon swung by a larger perpetrator."

Vic knelt beside him and gingerly pulled the suits back

near the wound. Dark spots were visible. "Phantasma," he muttered. "Black phantasma. These guys were in the most wrong place at a very bad time." He stood and looked at the factory. "I would say something about a lucky break but I'm not sure lucky is the right word at the moment."

Johnny stepped beside him. "Are we going to look closer or should I let the others know?"

"Go ahead and notify them. If he is in there, I doubt he's alone, kicking back, and listening to Pavarotti." The ghost dug in his pocket for the half-full cigarette pack he'd found in the glovebox. He took two out and offered the other to his partner after he finished his text. The young man looked at it before he shrugged and took it. Vic lit his and handed him the lighter. "Hey, kid, just to let you know it's been…" His voice trailed off as Johnny lit his cigarette and took a drag.

"Are you going from an optimist to a nihilist now?" the revenant asked. Vic looked at him in bemusement. "I'm only saying it sounds like you're about to go into some 'In case we don't win the day' speech."

"Humph." The ghost grunted and took a drag. "I was thinking along the lines of something nice like that, yeah. But I guess I can keep my trap shut."

Johnny chuckled and looked at the flickering light of his cigarette in the rapidly darkening sky. "Only because it isn't necessary."

Vic slid a hand into his jacket pocket. "You think so? Not to borrow your words, but when did you become such an optimist?"

"I'm more of a realist. I'm not saying we're guaranteed to win," he clarified and surprised his companion. "Or I guess I should say we aren't destined to survive. If the worse comes to the worst, the city will probably be smitten or something along those lines. I've heard so many worst-case scenarios in the last week that they all start to blur together. But one thing they all have in common is that the Axman doesn't win."

The ghost detective regarded his partner for a moment in silence. He took a long drag of his cigarette before smoke leaked out of his skull as he began to laugh. "That might be one of the dimmest silver linings I've ever heard, kid!" He laughed again and his hat almost fell off. "But I'm impressed. I guess you are right. We may all be taken out and New Orleans left as a crater, but at least he doesn't win."

"Well, death isn't the end," Johnny remarked with a smirk. "You are the nonliving proof of that."

"True," Vic agreed and looked at his skeletal hands. "But...I do wonder something."

He leaned against a tree, his cigarette half gone. "And what's that?"

"Given our bond, what do you think happens when you kick it?" he asked and pointed to each of them.

The revenant shrugged. "I don't know. I assumed that since I would be a ghost too you would get the part of yourself you gave me and I would be my own being again."

Vic sighed and placed his hand against his face. "Johnny, that's not possible. I had to give you part of my soul because you had part of yours taken. I don't think it grows back any more than a lost limb does."

"Oh." The young detective frowned and took another drag. "I guess we'll have to see how we can get it back then.

At least married couples only have to stick together until death do them part. I'm not saying you wouldn't be a good roommate for eternity but you know how it is."

"Yeah, yeah." Vic chortled, crushed his finished cigarette between his skeletal fingertips, and placed the remains in his inner pocket. "Well, however this goes, I guess we'll still have at least a few cases ahead of us, huh?"

Johnny responded with an easy smile. "Yeah, at least one more. Assuming we're right and we'll only be bonded instead of forced into some weird two-headed freak ghost."

His partner shook his head. "You had to ruin it, huh?"

He held his hands up defensively. "Hey, I'm only pointing out the possibility. We are about to face a guy who has kicked our asses in the last few days."

"Speaking of which, are they coming yet?" the ghost asked and made a phone gesture with his hand.

Johnny put his cigarette out and retrieved his phone. "No replies."

"I guess we'll have to wait a little longer before we move in," Vic suggested before a loud click broke the silence. They both hid quickly behind trees and watched as one of the large front doors of the factory opened. A figure shuffled out holding an ax. "Clone or real thing?"

The revenant squinted. "I would say clone given his buddy." He pointed behind the terror to another that wandered out after him.

"Buddies, it looks like," the ghost added when several more emerged from the shadows of the factory. "It doesn't look like they know we're here."

They took care to remain hidden as the beings crept

closer to the forest line and to them but stopped a short distance away and began to form lines.

"What are they doing?" Johnny asked and glanced at the corpses of the agents. "Maybe it wasn't the Axman who took them out. It might have been these guys."

"Still, there are a hell of a lot of them in a mostly abandoned area," Vic pointed out. "Even if the Axman isn't here himself, he certainly wants this place secured."

The revenant studied them as they stood lifelessly in rows in front of the factory. He couldn't decide if they were preparing to leave or merely standing guard. Several turned their heads and he ducked reflexively. The clones were at least manageable—shoot them enough and they eventually disappeared, albeit after a barrage or if they were hit by something with a little more punch to it. But this many at once was not a fight he and Vic could win alone.

Suddenly, one turned its head toward them. The partners pressed themselves behind their trees but the clones began to move and it now looked like they had no choice. Johnny reached for his gun as he glanced at the car. Maybe they had enough time to reach it and speed out before they could overwhelm them.

A bright purple flash made him freeze. Against his better judgment, he looked to see what it was. A hail of bullets poured through before a figure in samurai armor followed with a furious yell and sliced through two of the clones.

"What in the hell?" Vic exclaimed as two cars drove through the portal and Samedi lumbered through it before it closed.

"Oh, thank God." Johnny sighed with relief when he saw the keeper. "Or loa or whatever." He aimed at a clone missing its arm and ax and fired a large blast that removed its head. The cars stopped and their allies poured out quickly. Big Daddy and Shemar wielded shotguns and Valerie carried her revolver.

Marco cracked the knees of one of the clones before he turned and hammered its head while a ghost Johnny did not recognize bound another in ghostly chains before he ripped it apart. A group of clones attempted to jump the samurai before they were felled by a hail of bullets and lasers as a group of ghost mafia and agents joined the fight.

Samedi strolled casually to the factory as a gang of clones ran out of the entrance with their axes held high. He simply held a hand up and they stopped in their tracks before he snapped his fingers and they vanished. A figure stood beside the loa who Johnny did not expect to see.

"Annie?"

"Johnny!" Valerie called and ran to them. "Sorry about the delay. We had to make sure everything was okay at the station before we came. Are you good?"

He nodded. "We're doing very well now."

"Can you confirm the Axman is in the building?" Donovan asked as he approached the group. "We recovered a weapon we believe has enough power to end him in one shot."

"If that's true, it almost seems like a mercy," Vic muttered and looked at the dilapidated building. "We stumbled upon this place a couple of days ago. Given the Axman's mad plan, this seems like one of the only places— as far as we know anyway—where he could be hiding."

A barrage of fire erupted from a machine gun nearby as a mobster walked toward them. "So what you are saying is you aren't sure?" he asked and fired a quick shot into the clone on the ground. "Aren't you two supposed to be detectives?"

"This is Rick," Donovan told them. "He's a nice guy but a little cranky."

"Not as much as the don will be once he finds out the Axman ain't here," Rick muttered and glanced to where the mob leader yelled orders as he fired a shotgun into the stomach of another clone. "He's starting to get fairly bloodthirsty...phantasma thirsty. Whatever."

"I'm only saying we haven't confirmed anything," Vic stated. "We didn't have a chance to go and take a look before all these idiots appeared. There are probably even more in the building."

Johnny nudged Valerie. "Hey, who's the new ghost and what is Annie doing here?"

"The ghost is a witch named Castecka," she replied.

Suddenly, an arm draped over his shoulder. "Did someone call my name?" He spun and aimed his gun at her, but she chuckled and pushed it to the side. "Well, that's quite a forceful introduction. You don't need to worry about me, sweetheart. I'm as interested in seeing the Axman bite it as anyone else here."

He lowered his weapon. "Sorry. But that's good to hear though. What can you do?"

She inspected her fingernails. "I have several tricks since I'm nice and stygia-boosted. Teleportation between Limbo and here and controlling weak-willed spirits is my forte." She waggled her fingers at one of the clones. "I can't seem to get hold of these. They don't have a will at all—or rather, they are tied to the Axman's, which makes things trickier." The clone was quickly filled with holes by the agents. "Not that they last very long."

"And Annie?" Johnny asked Marco hurried to her and Samedi. "Will she be okay out here?"

Valerie sighed and shrugged. "She was insistent that she should come. Samedi promised to watch over her and said she would be better with us than stashed away at the precinct."

"And you agree with that?" Vic asked.

She nodded. "It stops the Axman from simply disappearing and taking her again like before."

The revenant frowned. "But wasn't she with you then too?"

The officer opened the chamber on her revolver and refilled it with ether rounds. "We're more cautious this time."

"We certainly got a good group going." Vic looked around the field. "They made short work of the clones out there. Hey, wasn't that huntsman with you?"

"Kaitō?" Johnny looked around. "I thought I saw him coming out of the portal. Where did he go?"

"I am going to enter the factory!" Samedi declared. "Be on guard. I feel the Axman's presence close by."

"Samedi, wait!" the ghost detective called. "Have you seen Kaitō? He didn't already go inside, did he?"

The loa looked back in concern but before he could speak, a body landed at their feet. It had fallen from high above. Johnny and Valerie ran to it and flipped it to reveal the very samurai they were looking for. His armor had multiple slashes and cracks and his face had become a monotone gray. "Kaitō?"

He struggled to his feet. "He is here…" He growled weakly and looked at the factory. "And he is not alone."

"Oh, but I am, huntsman!" a voice boomed from above. A figure stood at the edge of a cracked window, both familiar to Johnny and yet quite different. He had grown much bigger than he remembered and red markings now covered his face. White lights were still set in his sockets but were now surrounded by a red hue. He stared at all of them in contempt. "It is only me, myself, and I in here. It's merely that there is quite a lot of me." As if on cue, a deluge of clones ran past the Axman and leapt off the building. They descended like a dark waterfall onto the teams below.

Everyone prepared to fire but Samedi leapt back and held his hands in the air. Steams of purple light flowed upward and washed over the clones, who disappeared as the light continued to snake higher. The Axman watched it approach and held his ax up as red phantasma coated it. Moments before it threatened to consume him, he swung his weapon down and the wave was cut in two, divided by a red fissure.

The baron caught hold of Marco and Annie, jumped back, and yelled for everyone else to retreat. Valerie, Johnny, and Vic helped to move Kaitō as the Axman's strike cut through the soil and opened a large red fissure. An eerie howl filled the air.

"Donovan!" Rick called. "We should probably pop the trunk now."

The agent nodded and pushed hastily to his feet. "I'm on my way! Everyone, don't do anything stupid."

The samurai unbuckled the front of his armor, pulled it off, and revealed a flute strapped to a chain around his neck. He pulled it off and brought it to his mouth as their adversary floated down.

The Axman saw him move but didn't approach. Instead, he laughed and pointed at the wounded warrior. "Are you going to play us a little song, huntsman?" he asked.

Kaitō didn't retort and simply blew into the instrument. Everyone else stood ready for an attack or looked at one another and tried to decide if they should make the first move. The warrior pulled himself up and Johnny helped to steady him as he sank his blade into the ground for balance. "I have called all my remaining brethren here, monster!" he called. "What hope do you have against the full might of the Wild Hunt?"

The Axman rested his weapon over his shoulder. He looked at the darkened sky and dozens of figures that moved toward them. "I must admit to a little lie," he began and returned his attention to the group. "It is hardly the darkest of my sins, but you were right, samurai." He held a hand up and placed his thumb against his middle finger. "I am not alone, not in this city."

He snapped his fingers but nothing happened. Johnny was ready for a renewed fight but none of the remaining clones reformed and no new ones appeared, so perhaps it was only a bluff.

"Oh, shit!" Big Daddy cried and pointed into the sky. "Behind us—back in the city!"

The group took a moment to turn—perhaps not the best tactic given how close the Axman was—but what they saw almost shocked them as much as his new appearance.

Large black pillars ascended from within the city. At first, the revenant thought they were creations made of phantasma, but they were hordes of shades and shadows that sprang up from all over the city and massed together before they turned and moved toward them.

"No!" Kaitō shouted and quickly took to the air toward his comrades. The other members of the Wild Hunt turned and saw the terrors approach. All were now focused on the oncoming swarm as blasts from SEA agents and their cannons launched a barrage through the sky.

"Oh, my my." The Axman smiled and looked eagerly at one of the group. "Hello again, Annie. I should probably be more infuriated that you ran from me not too long ago, but I have to admit that merely seeing your pretty face is quite delightful. Having you already here will make the process so much easier."

"What the hell is the matter with this guy?" Johnny muttered, his weapon trained on the murderer. "I know he's a psychopath but I got more of a Dracula vibe from him before. Now, he seems like a banana peel away from sounding like a straight lunatic."

"He is starting to sound like Kriminel," Vic concurred. "He absorbed his essence. My guess is that it's screwing with whatever sanity he had left. I don't know if that makes him more or less dangerous."

"Axman!" Samedi intoned and approached the dark figure. "You will harm no more of us today."

Their adversary chuckled and nodded at the sky and the battle between his terrors and the Wild Hunt. "You might want to do something quickly if you want to keep that promise."

Suddenly, the loa disappeared, surprising everyone including the killer, only for him to appear at his side and ready to throw a punch. The Axman held his ax up to block him but even with it between him and the keeper's fist, he was launched back into the wall of the factory.

He sat up quickly and adjusted his skull. "Well then, it's fine by me. You are the last thing in my way, Keeper." He lifted his ax and it began to glow red. "I'll make this entire field the same color as my phantasma." He lunged and swung. Samedi danced out of its path but a wave of phantasma launched in the weapon's wake.

One of the mobsters grasped Don Pesci and flew out of the way as the wave cut through two agents and several mobsters. Annie dragged Marco to the ground and Rick and Donovan were forced to drop the crate they carried as everyone else scrambled to safety.

When they looked up, the Axman slashed at Samedi and launched more waves—vertical, horizontal, and diagonal to keep them pinned. The loa was finally able to catch the blade. Purple phantasma burst from his palm as he kicked his opponent down and prepared to sink his fist into his chest.

The Axman raised his other arm and dark, inky tendrils spat from it. They ensnared the keeper and held him aloft.

"Don't just sit there, you idiots!" Pesci yelled out and snatched his shotgun up. "We came here to blast this bastard back to where he belongs, so let's do it!" He, his men, and anyone else with a gun began to fire and, their salvos struck seemingly every inch of his body. The Axman turned and scowled, lifted his ax again, and coated it with red phantasma.

Samedi uttered a war cry, snapped the dark tendrils that bound him, and blasted his foe away in an explosion of purple light. The killer floated, his attention torn between the loa and the annoyances who continued to fire at him. He slammed into the dirt and created a series of fissures along the field. An agent fell through one that formed beneath her while the ghosts were dragged toward them.

"Where the hell is it taking us?" Big Daddy demanded.

"I'm not interested in finding out!" Castecka held her hands up and created sigils in the sky before she placed her hands together and the sigils exploded. Lines began to form over the crevasses, then enlarged and covered them. The witch's full appearance began to wither, her cheeks sank in, and her smooth hair began to fray as her green color dulled.

Rick and Donovan had finally found their chance, opened the crate quickly, and hauled the weapon out. "We're gonna need a clean shot," the mobster warned as his companion replaced the ammo. "So that means get the hell out of the way. There's a wide splash zone!"

Johnny began to feel that there wasn't more they could do besides stay out of the way. He watched Samedi and the Axman continue their fight and hadn't realized how much the loa had been drained by everything. The baron had ripped his brother's crux out of him so easily, but his attacks now almost seemed like little more than a brawl.

But it appeared to be a brawl he could win—something the killer seemed to notice as he constantly tried to dodge and block more hits than take them directly. At least, that's what it looked like, but when Samedi reeled back to blast the monster, the Axman rushed him. The baron launched a blast that his adversary took in its entirety, which allowed him to drive his ax into the loa's chest.

Samedi did not cry out. Instead, he lifted his leg and kicked his foe several yards back. The killer pushed to his feet and smiled wickedly as the baron tried to pry the ax out of his chest.

Johnny heard a hum and crackle in the air and turned to where Donovan and Rick prepared to fire the cannon they had brought. A bright blue light glowed around them. Their target turned and noticed them. The red in his eyes darkened as he prepared to run at them, but he stopped as the agent fired and held his arm out.

Everyone watched in horror as the Axman called his namesake to him with Samedi still attached. He caught it and ripped the weapon out of the keeper's chest, then kicked him forward into the path of the blast.

CHAPTER TWENTY-THREE

The eruption covered almost the entire field. Johnny and Vic fused and took cover behind a tree. Even outside the direct path of the blast, it felt like he had been hit by lightning that tried to make his body combust, and he heard Vic try to muffle a shout of pain.

The revenant fell to his knees as the light and explosion subsided, then crawled quickly into the clearing. He froze when he came across a large dull and ashen hand. A withered moan drew his attention to the baron. The lights in his eyes were dim and blue burns coated his body.

"Samedi!" He gasped and Vic reappeared and helped him prop the keeper up.

"How do you feel, big guy?" the ghost asked as the baron hung his head.

"It does not matter," he muttered and attempted to get to his feet before he collapsed and clutched the ax wound in his chest. "I must fight. Where is the Axman?"

That was a very good question. Even if he hadn't been hit directly, he must have been caught in the aftermath.

Johnny looked around but didn't see the killer. He looked at the others and saw some of them recovering, Donovan knelt next to Rick and reached into a compartment on his belt.

"I have some stygia for you," the agent revealed to the weakened ghost. "Why you didn't let me get one of my agents to do this is beyond me."

The mobster rolled his graying head to look at him. "Like I was going to miss the opportunity to be one of those who iced the Axman." He groaned, his hands limp at his side. "We didn't even hit him, the son of a bitch. Did we at least wound the bastard?"

"I think we forced him to retreat," Donovan told him and popped the top of the vial. "He's gone for now."

"Gone? He ain't running at a time like—shit! Donovan move!" Rick mustered all the strength he could and used the last of his tangibility to push him back and an ax descended and sliced the mobster in two.

"Rick!" the agent shouted, readied his rifle quickly, and aimed it upward. The Axman floated only a few yards above them, the entire right half of his body a dark-gray skeleton. The dark phantasma attempted to coat it, and his eyes were a very violent hue of red.

"So that was your last gasp?" he questioned, the cruel mirth in his voice gone and replaced by a chilling, wrathful tone. "I have to give you credit. It was certainly more effective than anything you've thrown at me so far."

He growled as he looked at his skeletal hand. Suddenly, he dove onto the cannon and it shattered under him. "But it and your loa guardian are both broken." He lifted his ax as Donovan fired as many shots as his rifle would let him before it overheated. The agent braced for the attack as their adversary stepped on his chest. "I have won!" he shouted and swung his ax as an explosion detonated beside him.

The blast was enough for the man to pry himself free and retreat behind one of the overturned cars. The Axman roared and lashed out with a slice of red phantasma in the direction from which the explosive had been thrown.

Donovan heard a familiar voice cry out. "Anderson!" he shouted and vented his rifle as he retrieved two explosives and tossed them at the killer.

"Is anyone still good to burn his ass already?" Pesci demanded and he, Big Daddy, and Shemar all unloaded on the target as the explosions went off.

"What is happening?" Samedi asked and tried to lean up to see.

"The Axman is still kicking," Vic informed him and attempted to get him to lie down. "We're not done fighting. None of us are."

The loa looked at his chest. "Tenacity will not win the day." He sighed and looked at Johnny. "Let me see your gun."

The revenant drew it quickly and handed it to the baron. He placed it along his wound and his purple phantasma began to seep into it. "I will see this to the end. I promised you that," he said as the lights in his eyes grew darker. "But I cannot fight alongside you now. Still, there is enough power in this for the Axman to feel it."

"Will it obliterate him?" the ghost detective asked as Samedi handed it back.

The loa turned away. "I'm sorry, but I cannot say so

with confidence." A moment later, he turned back and caught the young detective's arm. "The girl—she is our last hope."

"Annie?" Johnny placed his hand on the baron's chest. "We'll protect her, don't worry."

The baron shook his head. "She does not want protection and if you want to end this, she needs to fight!" he demanded.

"I don't know what you are talking about, Baron," the revenant told him and studied the gun. "We'll find another way to end this, all right?"

The keeper lay back again and looked at the sky. "It is getting very dark now. You must send the Axman back to Hell for light to return."

Vic heard cries coming from the fighting behind them. "He certainly deserves to rot for eternity but at this point, I would be all right with simply obliterating the bastard."

His partner grimaced. "Besides, we're in this mess because he found a way to escape." They would need to find the deepest, darkest pit they could if they wanted to finally be rid of this menace. He froze when he realized that he knew where a deep, dark pit could be found. Quickly, he flipped his eyepatch up, looked around, and cursed when he couldn't see any crossing points.

"What's the matter, kid?" the ghost detective asked. "Do you have an idea?"

Johnny hesitated for a moment and focused on the gun. They couldn't rely on it killing the Axman, but Samedi had said he would certainly feel it and that might be enough. He holstered the weapon and looked at his partner. "Do you remember when I was a kid and I asked you all kinds of questions about being a ghost?"

Vic tilted his head in confusion. "Well...yeah. You wouldn't shut up about it for a couple of years, but is this the time to reminisce?"

The revenant closed his eyes for a moment. "Remember when I asked what happened when a ghost was obliterated and you said that they were simply gone?" He opened them again and stared into his companion's lights. "I said that seemed very scary and you told me that in some ways, you wouldn't mind as long as your last thought was of something good." The ghost opened his mouth to respond but it remained open for a moment before he closed it and nodded. "Would destroying that son of a bitch be good enough?"

His partner adjusted his hat and stood. "You're damn right it would." For a moment, his hard exterior broke and Johnny saw concern in his face. "But what about you, kid?"

Johnny shrugged and smiled reassuringly at him. "Well, if what you said is true, then I won't have to worry about it all that much after it's over, right?" He stood and turned away. "Besides, I'm a better fool than I am an investigator but at least I can go as a proud one." His gaze scanned the field until he located the ghost he was looking for. "Assuming the witch can punch us a ticket."

CHAPTER TWENTY-FOUR

The Axman upended a car and swung viciously to continue his onslaught. Marco and several others tried to beat him back, but he barreled through them, sliced through two more mobsters, and hacked into Marco's ribs. He fell with a gasp of shock and when he released his bat, the blue flames died.

"Marco!" Annie shouted and drew the enemy's attention.

He turned to her, his eyes full of rage. "No more deals and no trickery." He seethed as he approached her. "You are the key, girl, and I will use you as my vessel." More spectral gunfire and explosions followed but at this point, he was well beyond caring.

Castecka began to sketch sigils into the dirt. She had no tricks that could hurt or stop the killer at this point, but maybe she could get Annie out of there and delay the end a little longer. A hand settled on her shoulder and she spun and frowned at Johnny.

"You said you were an expert at teleportation between here and Limbo right?" he demanded. She was so startled that all she could do was nod. "How accurate are you?"

"Why?" she asked. "There isn't much time but I can still—"

"Can you send us and the Axman to Limbo?"

"He'll simply come back!"

He placed his hands on her shoulders. "I promise you that if you can get us to the edge of Limbo, he will not."

"The edge?" She gaped when realization dawned on her. "Are you crazy? I can probably make a portal there but I can't hold it open for long. You'll be trapped with him."

"We're well aware of that," Vic replied. "You said you wanted him gone as much as all of us. Well, here's your chance."

Castecka stared at them but a roar from the Axman made her snap out of it. "Fine, but I can't get it too close or it would simply suck everyone in with you." With a sigh, she looked down at her partially completed sigil. "You had better not mess this up." She quickly scratched out the marker she had made and began a new one. "I'll open the portal behind him. It's the best I can do. You'll have to trip him or something."

Johnny drew his gun, which glowed purple. "I have a better plan than that."

"Annie!" the killer shouted and continued to swipe at her while everyone attempted to slow him. "You cannot and will not stop this, girl!" The revenant prepared to bolt toward him as soon as the witch opened the portal, but Annie stopped running, turned to face the enemy, and pressed her hands together.

"What the hell is she doing?" Vic shouted and looked at Castecka. "How much longer?"

"Only a moment," she replied and glanced at the scene. "I'm not sure she has it, though."

The young detective held a hand out. "Give me your gun!" he instructed and Vic complied before he fused with him. Johnny ran to the side of the Axman and began to fire the pistol at their adversary's head. The psychopath turned and swiped violently, and he ducked under the attack while the killer regarded him with contempt. "You! You damn nuisance!" He hissed in fury and launched another onslaught that Johnny had to dodge. "You ruined my plans! My dream would have been accomplished by now if you hadn't come along and ruined it. And for what? A paycheck!"

A portal begin to open behind the Axman as he marched toward him. The revenant drew his gun and holstered Vic's. "I guess I know how to earn it," he retorted and fired a shot. His adversary walked into it, expecting it to be merely another ether shot, but it hurled him back and into the portal. He uttered a surprised, angry cry as he fell through. Johnny ran to the portal and looked at Annie with a smile. "You deserve a normal life after all this," he shouted as he raced past her. "Enjoy it, all right?"

"Johnny?" Her voice was a mixture of confusion and worry as the young detective threw himself into the portal and fired another shot at the Axman as he tried to run out again. The blast flung him farther down the cracked cobbled street they were on. When the killer scrambled to his feet, he stumbled back. He looked over his shoulder and the gaping maw of the Big Dark stared at him.

"Do you think a pathetic trick like this will be the—" The young detective fired a shot into his mouth and cut him off as it thrust him farther back. The killer managed to sink his skeletal fingers into a damaged pillar to stop himself.

Johnny realized he was being dragged down the road and shifted to the side. He was able to grasp a streetlight and tried to line up another shot on the enemy, who pulled himself up the road.

"How many shots do you think you have left?" Vic asked.

"I'll make it enough," he replied, released the post, and bounded to the other side. He was immediately dragged down the street and toward the Axman. The killer was so incensed that he let go of the wall he was holding onto so he could strike but the pull of the abyss made him miss his swing.

Johnny struck him feet first before he blasted him with another shot. It catapulted the killer several yards ahead of them but they both slid toward the edge of Limbo. The Axman was at the precipice when he slammed his weapon into the street to stop himself, but his hold was tenuous.

Vic unfused and caught hold of another streetlight. He grasped the back of his partner's jacket and held on tightly as the young man lined his shot up, pulled the trigger, and caught his target in the shoulder. The strike jerked the ax out and launched it and him into the darkness. The weapon flew past its owner, but the killer extended his hand and tendrils of his dark phantasma emerged to wind around Johnny's leg.

"Gah!" He heaved as it felt like his leg would be torn off. "This petty jackass!"

Vic was stretched as far as he could go. "I can't hold on much longer, kid!" he warned.

The revenant looked back. "Well, we came into this knowing it could be the end of the line." He tried to plant his other foot down to slow them. "At least we'll go out hearing him curse our names."

His partner's eyes glimmered. "I've been called many imaginative things in my time. I hope he at least makes it fun."

Johnny chuckled and prepared to give Vic the word when he saw the Axman begin to pull on the tendrils to crawl out, but someone else called his name. He felt a pang of fear as he looked up the street. "Annie?"

"Annie?" the ghost echoed and scowled at the girl, who held onto the walls as she moved closer to them. "What are you doing here? Get back—this will swallow you whole!"

She nodded but did the opposite, released her hold, and floated down the street to catch hold of the other side of the streetlight. "I can't let you do this!" she shouted over the howling pull of the vortex.

"What are you talking about?" Johnny grunted with the strain of the Axman's weight on his leg. "We're big boys and are perfectly capable of sacrificing ourselves if we so choose."

"Not when I can do something about it." She held a closed hand out and opened it to reveal a small white orb. "Use this on him, Johnny!" she demanded.

Vic looked at it, then at his partner before he adjusted

his grip on the lamp post and tried to pull Johnny closer. The revenant holstered his gun and stretched to take the orb. Annie leaned forward and he was able to catch it between the tips of his fingers. He looked down and realized that the Axman had made it to the street and now glared at the group before he noticed the orb in Johnny's hand.

The detective focused on the phantasma wound around his leg and thrust the orb into it. It burst apart, coated the phantasma, and began to overtake it. In moments, it surged down the webbing and toward the killer to ensnare his fingers first, then wind around his whole arm and across his shoulders.

The Axman tried to brush it off but it jumped to his other hand, consumed it, and began to move through the other side of his body. Johnny wasn't sure what it was doing to him but it was clear the killer didn't like it. He began to panic and uttered a stream of shouts, croaks, and curses as the white phantasma began to consume him and strip him of the dark phantasma. The dark tendrils around his leg broke apart and the killer slid down the street again. He tried to make them grab something else but they were now brittle and weak and shattered around the pillar he tried to attach to.

He finally uttered a desperate shriek as he was reduced to the skeleton he had been before. No longer strong enough to fight the power of the abyss, he was lifted and carried into the dark.

Johnny drew his gun again and max'd the power, yelled at Vic to grab Annie, and charged a shot. He fired and it hurled the three back only a few feet but enough to catch hold of a windowsill that began to crumble due to the weight. It held long enough for him to charge another shot and fire to drive them farther. A large metal mailbox gave them an opportunity to plant their feet and brace against the vacuum so they could drag themselves up the street.

They covered several yards, each of them holding different parts of buildings to keep them steady, the revenant looked back as the Axman drifted deeper into the maw. He expected him to be pulled farther until there was nothing left to see and nowhere for him to go, but his eyes widened when a massive claw appeared out of the darkness and snatched the killer.

The young detective was too stunned to say anything but briefly saw the Axman struggle in its grasp before he turned with a wail of terror that was barely audible over the howl of the Big Dark. The scream signified not only fear but the knowledge of what awaited him. Johnny's eyes widened and he could have sworn he saw a massive creature smiling deep within as the killer was suddenly dragged out of sight.

"Johnny!" Vic shouted and he snapped back to reality. He glanced to where the ghost held Annie several yards ahead. "Come on, partner! One last push." The revenant nodded, shoved against the half-crumbled structure, and inched around it to the other side. He planted his feet on it and thrust off. His friends caught him and dragged him along as they continued up the street.

Finally, after what felt like hours but couldn't have been more than several minutes, they were far enough away that while they could still feel the pull, it didn't threaten to suck them into the abyss. They pushed forward to extend the distance between them and the edge until Johnny gestured to what looked like an old cathedral. He and Vic pushed the doors open and they collapsed inside.

"All right," the ghost stated, the first to stand while his companions had to take a moment. "Anyone who isn't dead, clap their hands." Annie made a small attempt to do so but Johnny only held up a shaking middle finger. "I guess that means Annie's the only one who gets a prize once we get back."

The revenant ran his hands over his head. "Hell, the only reason we get to go back is because of her." He sat and helped her up. "Thank you, Annie. I wasn't kidding about that sacrifice, though."

She smiled and rested her head against the wall. "I thought you would try something like that. I didn't want another death because of me."

Vic slid his hand into his pocket. "Eh, to be honest, we merely wanted that dick gone and dusted as much as we wanted to help you." He took his cigarette pack out and scowled when he realized the contents were crushed. "Dammit."

Annie nodded and turned to Johnny. "I didn't get a chance to see but he's gone now, right? For sure?"

He looked out of one of the broken windows to the Big Dark and recalled what he had seen. His first thought was to ask if either of them had seen what he had but since they both looked expectantly at him, he knew they had not. He took a moment to consider telling them every detail but realized that they had been through enough thus far. Vic could hear about it later but for now, he tried to get the image out of his head.

"Yeah, he's gone," he said with a satisfied nod. "There's nowhere to go for him now but deeper into the dark."

Vic adjusted his hat. "I guess he'll have time to devise another scheme, assuming he isn't obliterated." He eased to the floor and stretched flat. "Good luck getting that going, though. No keeper or anyone else will venture into the Big Dark." Johnny had to agree. Given what he had seen, there was a good chance no one would get very far anyway.

Annie craned her neck to look outside. "Say…um, now that it is all over, how do we get back?" She turned to them with an anxious frown. "The portal closed after I dove in."

The revenant pointed to his eye. "We'll find a crossing point, although there's no guarantee that it'll take us to New Orleans. We might have to hop on a bus."

"Do you have cash on you?" Vic asked.

The young man nodded and eased himself against the wall. "Yeah, I can buy a couple of tickets. Hopefully, we can at least find one that's still in the south and save on fare." He yawned and let his head hang. "Maybe we'll get lucky and stumble on a ferryman. He might give us a deal for saving reality and all that jazz."

Vic considered this. "You know, the ferryman who took us to the Wild Hunt's island offered us a ride back. Maybe he wouldn't mind a reroute."

"It sounds good to me," Johnny muttered and slid closer to sleep. "Give me a few minutes and we can go."

"We should probably get back asap and see—" The ghost cut himself off when he saw that Annie was already dozing and his partner wasn't far behind. He straightened and studied them. Sleep was something he'd hated back when he was alive since it always demanded he take it at the worst times when he was on the job. But he did have to admit to the satisfaction of having a good rest after a job was completed.

The world—both of them—could wait for a spell.

CHAPTER TWENTY-FIVE

"In the week since the devastation of our town, we have made great progress," the mayor of New Orleans declared from the television screen. "With the labor and financial assistance of the SEA and the help of both the generosity and resilient spirits of NOLA's children, we have begun to return to the normalcy we all desire. Well, as much as anything in this strange and magnificent city can be called normal."

"I'm not sure this is the time for jokes like that," Shemar grumbled as he continued to read the reports. "There is still considerable work to do."

Valerie placed a cup of coffee on his table. "Yeah, but you have to admit that it is true." She sipped from her cup. "Even when we get back to the ways things were—or as close to it as possible after everything that happened—it's not like the normal everyone else knows." She looked at the front window of his office. "I have to say, despite how much the Agency bungled things during that whole mess, they have good contractors."

"Honestly, I simply wish they were gone by this point." The police captain sighed. "But I guess they are doing well to at least try to make up for their mistakes." He glanced at her. "Has Donovan told you what's happening with Lovett?"

The officer moved to the window and shook her head. "Since he's still here and helping with the rebuilds and any remaining terror cases, he's not that much in the loop. All he knows is that she hasn't been seen at their headquarters since she was recalled after the barrier went down."

"Humph. With how these things work, she'll be let go quietly with a severance package—assuming they don't shuffle her elsewhere." He tossed a file to the side, rubbed his head, and put the thought away. "Ah, well. It's nothing I need to be concerned about right now. How's the rest of the station?"

She slid a finger across the new glass. "The station is almost completely repaired. An odd paint job or two still needs to get done but it is almost like this place wasn't attacked by any terrors at all."

Shemar began to type. "I wish that was how it is for filing. I don't think we've ever been this busy."

"At least new cases have dwindled," she reminded him as she sat. "Then again, that's after the massive spike we had over the last few months so the graph is a little skewed." She sighed and placed her coffee on the desk. "Seriously, sir, you've been cooped up in here for almost a month now."

"It hasn't been that long. I've taken showers."

"In the locker room!" she pointed out and folded her arms. "The city may still be picking up the pieces but it ain't going to fall apart now. You can take a break." She received no response from him and rolled her eyes. "Are you at least coming to the parade?"

"That's today?" he asked and looked slightly startled. "How did they get it together so fast?"

"People want to party," she replied bluntly. "We know there's still a long road ahead and things are gonna change, but a brief reprieve will make that all go down easier."

He seemed to consider it for a moment before he turned to his computer. "The meeting with Pesci was moved to tomorrow so I guess I do have a little time."

Valerie frowned. "Do you honestly think it will hold? The mafia will probably go back to their old ways soon."

"I have no doubt about that. Not everyone will fall in line, but the don said he intended to change things. He claims that if they were run better, they would have dealt with the situation before it got out of hand. If we can curb any future incidents and he's serious about changing things here, I want to at least try to take the opportunity." He looked at the TV screen. "The mayor will join us too, so try to keep it hush-hush."

She sighed and picked her coffee up. "That won't help any conspiracy theories in the future," she muttered and took a sip. "I saw Castecka earlier and asked her about Aiyana."

Shemar paused and looked at her. "How is she?"

"She said she couldn't find her and that her name wasn't even on the ledger of arrivals in Limbo." She allowed herself a small smile. "It seems like she was destined for a better place than Limbo, same as Grandma."

He leaned back and nodded. "She would always talk

about those spirits of hers and how kind and benevolent they were. I hope they recognized that when her time came." He looked at her. "We haven't talked much about anything other than work in a while. Are you all right, baby?"

Valerie sighed contently. "I'm fine, Pops. I don't think I'll volunteer for any big cases in the near future but I'm ready when you need me."

"You say that and yet you're here when you're supposed to be on leave," he remarked dryly. "I thought you would go to see Johnny and Vic off."

"They'll swing by later." She took another sip. "They wanted to make a stop first to say goodbye to some other friends or something."

"Where?"

She shrugged and crossed one leg over the other. "It's not a place I'm familiar with. I think they said it was called The Carnivale."

"Romeo, another," Vic said, holding up his empty mug.

"Coming right up," the barkeep called as he handed out a tray of shots to other patrons. He took the empty mug, filled it, and thumped it on the bar with a loud slap.

"Hey, man. You're spilling it everywhere!" The ghost detective yelped.

"It's all right. I'll get you however much you need." Romeo laughed and looked around the full lounge. "Now that people are coming in to drink instead of simply using the portal in the can, I can afford it." He leaned closer and prodded him in the chest. "And that's thanks to you, good sir."

"Me and the kid," Vic corrected and looked back to where Johnny was surrounded by other ghosts, who asked him all kinds of questions. "I don't think he's used to this whole celebrity status."

The proprietor laughed. "Well, you are both the men of the hour. Plus him being a living revenant is still a novelty."

"That and most other ghosts know I don't mind smacking anyone who invades my personal space." He took out and lit a cigarette. "We're heading out later and wanted to say that you've got a good place going, Romeo. We're gonna miss it."

"Well, don't be a stranger," the owner demanded. "There is always a seat for you here and free drinks—within reason."

"Heh, don't worry about that. A guy like me got over drowning his sorrows before he kicked it." He gulped half the mug. "The kid starts to feel woozy after too much anyway and he still needs to drive."

"Oh, is he your chauffeur too, Vic?" The detective and barkeep looked at a large purple ghost in a well-tailored suit. "Howdy, gentleman."

"Big Daddy." They both greeted him as he puffed on his trademark cigar.

"What brings you here?" Vic asked.

"Honestly, I came through to see Catherine again. But as for why I dropped by, I'm merely the messenger today." He jerked his thumb to the outside. "Someone would like to exchange pleasantries with you and the kid."

The detective tilted his head. "Can't they come in here themselves?"

He chortled and removed his cigar from his jaw. "Let's say it would cause something of a ruckus."

Vic took the hint and drained the last of his drink. "We wouldn't want that, especially with the bar just opening," he conceded as he slid off his seat. "See you around, Romeo."

"Won't you come back?"

He shook his head. "Nah, we gotta get out of town anyway—keep the new legend alive and all that." He looked at Johnny and whistled despite his lack of lips. "Hey, kid! We got something!"

"Coming!" the revenant responded, excused himself from the crowd, and hurried toward him. "Good Lord, Vic. I've tried to signal you to get me out of there for ten minutes now."

His partner laughed and clapped him on the back. "Hey, maybe next time, we can charge them per minute. We'd make a mint fairly quickly." He nodded at Big Daddy. "Come on. It looks like we have a special guest."

The group wandered out of the bar and cheers and well wishes followed them. When they exited, a limo awaited them and a ghostly chauffeur opened the door. "It looks like business is still good, Marsan," Vic noted.

"Are you kidding? After it was revealed that my clients helped to deal with the Axman, people have come to me with all kinds of gigs." The dealer beamed. "I only wish you could have saved me a trophy or something."

The ghost detective rolled his eyes as they entered the vehicle. "Yeah, we'll think about that next time."

They settled in the lush violet interior and noticed someone else waiting for them. The partners almost didn't recognize him at first but the exotic suit and cane corrected that quickly. "Baron Samedi?" Johnny asked.

The loa leaned forward. He was gaunt but all smiles and the light had returned to his eyes. "Hello, gentlemen."

"You look a little scrawny there, Baron," Vic commented and took a drag of his cigarette. "But it's good to see you moving around again."

The keeper chuckled and nodded as he straightened. "Catherine has watched over me. It is good to be a demigod with many believers still around. And I have had a chance to return to my domain since the destruction of the Axman. Little by little, I return to my former glory and I can at least put this terrible business in the past."

"Are you able to sort souls still?" the revenant asked.

He held a hand up and shook it. "The other keepers have helped me with that. Many are now aware of what transpired but I'll probably have to deal with that soon."

"Will they pin you to the wall?" Vic asked.

Samedi shrugged. "I am not worried about that for now. I am prepared for whatever happens, but the fact that the situation has been dealt with will probably work in my favor." He nodded and pointed his cane at them. "And I have you to thank for that."

The partners shared a look. "You sure do," the ghost detective agreed. "Next time, post a gig like a normal person, all right?"

"Yes." The loa responded with a rueful laugh. "But hopefully, I won't need you for something so dire. Maybe simply a nice chat. I like to think of us as friends now."

Johnny shrugged. "It certainly couldn't hurt to have a keeper on our side."

Vic held a finger up warningly. "You say that but it could be trouble."

The revenant fixed him with an almost disbelieving gaze. "Vic, our life is usually defined by trouble."

"Okay, that's a fair point."

The baron and Big Daddy laughed. Samedi undid a couple of buttons on his shirt. "Another person who helped me was our dear Annie," he revealed and showed them one of the areas that had been burned in the blast, which had healed. "She has come a long way with her empath. It's a very powerful thing."

The ghost detective considered this for a long moment. "Will it make her a target in the future?" he asked, thinking of the consequences. "I saw what it did to the Axman and if it can heal a keeper, many people will want something like that for themselves."

"That is why we shall keep it a secret," Samedi replied and buttoned his shirt. "I don't believe she plans to do anything that will require the use of her powers in normal circumstances. She and her brother merely want to get on with their lives."

"I don't blame them," Johnny agreed and looked out the window. "We'll leave soon and swing by the station. They are supposed to meet us there before we head out."

"Are you going on another gig already?" Big Daddy asked and puffed on his cigar. "I don't remember being told that you picked something up."

Vic shook his head. "We need to head home for a while.

New Orleans is a nice place but the kid barely sees his own bed as it is."

The dealer nodded. "Well, if you need something, let me know."

"I'm sure we'll be by soon enough." The revenant adjusted the strap of his eyepatch. "We'll get bored of having it easy soon enough."

Samedi laughed and the feathers on his back shook. "You have some special spirits. You know, Kaitō told me that the Wild Hunt is looking for more members to fill their ranks. Maybe there will be a place for you when the time comes."

Johnny pulled a concerned face. "Thanks for the thought but I'm not the military type."

"Same," Vic said as he stubbed his cigarette out in the limo's ashtray. "Besides, I like working with a partner, not a platoon."

"I'll pass that along," the baron said as he reached into his pocket and withdrew a card. "Here. Take this. If you ever need me, burn it and I'll be there." Vic took it and the loa looked at his skeletal fingers. "I would hold off on it for a little while, though. I'll be more use to you after a little more rest. Well, that and assuming the other keepers aren't still arguing over what to do with me."

The ghost detective studied the card, which displayed a picture of the keeper standing over a grave with a shovel in his hand, tipping his top hat. "Samedi, before we go, there is something I want to ask."

"Anything. Go on."

"When we were hunting Kriminel, we came across one of your gravesites," he began and passed the card to Johnny.

"One of them was marked for Annie." The baron tensed but nodded. "Were you planning, if things went south, to fill her grave prematurely?"

Samedi closed his eyes and nodded. "I had opened the grave before I contacted you. Once I found out what Kriminel wanted to accomplish, it felt like the simplest way to solve the problem."

The young man placed the card in his jacket pocket. "I wasn't happy when I saw it, but I understand why you did it." He looked down for a moment before he turned to the loa. "So what made you change your mind?"

The baron opened his eyes. "It was the difference between me and my brother. Life and death have a purpose and existence is worth preserving. If there was a chance to spare the girl and still end the calamity, I had to take it."

"And do you feel it was worth it?" Vic asked when everyone went silent for a moment aside from the occasional drag from Big Daddy's cigar.

Samedi looked away for a moment. "I do. Much was lost but not forever."

"Even the ghosts who were obliterated?" the ghost detective asked and folded his arms. "I'm very sure that's final."

"Is that so?" Samedi replied with a smirk. "I guess that lie still holds weight."

"Excuse me?"

He waved him off. "Never you mind for now. The dead will be honored. That is my role, after all. Existence moves on and we should enjoy that." He pulled a watch from his jacket pocket. "I need to return to my domain. I'm glad we could see each other again."

Johnny moved down the seat and extended a hand. "They were odd circumstances and all, but thanks for your help, Baron."

Vic sighed, leaned forward, and shook Samedi's hand after Johnny was done. "Same, although it was your fault to begin with." His partner knocked him on the shoulder as he leaned back. "What?"

The loa took it with good humor, closed the pocket watch, and put it away. "I'll try to make sure to not trouble you in the future."

The ghost detective held his hands up in mock outrage. "Don't do that. Simply make it less than the world ending and we can work with it."

Samedi tipped his hat to him as purple smoke began to fill the car. "I'll keep it in mind. Best wishes to you, friends." Big Daddy opened the windows and when the smoke cleared, the loa was gone.

Vic waved a few vapors out of his face. "At least his flair for the dramatic seems to be intact."

"For good or bad," Johnny added.

The dealer stubbed his cigar out. "All right, gentlemen. Where can I take you?"

"We appreciate it, Marsan, but we got our own ride." Vic waved him off.

"Oh right, right." He adjusted his suit, tapped the window, and the door opened. "Well, I know I'll see you soon, so it's probably best to not have a melodramatic goodbye."

Vic shook his head as he and Johnny moved past him to the door. "You could at least be a little courteous about it, though."

Big Daddy opened a compartment next to him, took a handful of cigars out, and passed them to the ghost on his way out. "Did I hurt your feelings? Will these make it better?"

"Oh." He took the cigars and nodded approvingly. "It's a good start. But cash would also be acceptable."

"I agree." The statement made the two turn back in surprise after they had stepped out. But instead of handing them a bag or case, the door closed and the window began to roll up. "I'll make sure to have something nice and juicy lined up for you when you come." He laughed as the window shut and the limo drove around the corner.

"Cheeky bastard," Vic muttered and shoved the cigars into his pocket.

"Well, we did technically steal his money not that long ago," Johnny reminded him as they moved toward their car.

"We were set up to do that," Vic countered. "Come on. Let's go see some people who appreciate us."

The revenant nodded as they approached the car and he pressed the unlock button. "Right, then. We'll head on out." He paused at the door and leaned against the vehicle. "It's kind of weird to think we made it through, huh?"

His partner stopped himself from ghosting through and looked at him. "You're starting to sound like a real detective now," he replied with a smirk. "I said that to myself countless times after my cases."

"Do you ever get used to it?"

The ghost shrugged. "Eh, a little, but you never want it to go away fully. It's a sign that you are still alive." He slipped into the car. "Besides, it makes the alcohol taste better."

When they arrived at the station, Valerie, Marco, and Annie waited for them at the front entrance. Johnny pulled up across the street, stepped out, and fed the meter before they hurried to the building.

"You're jaywalking, you know." Valerie pointed out. "Make sure you keep that in mind the next time you do that across from a police officer who isn't your friend."

"We got off without even a warning?" Johnny laughed as he hugged her and Annie and shook Marco's hand.

"Or a bribe," Vic added and received a wry smirk from Valerie as they hugged. "How are all of you doing?"

"Fairly good," Marco said as he lifted his shirt and revealed the large amount of gauze around his chest. "It only required, like, thirty stitches. Can you believe that?"

"Well, it was mostly a graze as I recall," Johnny commented.

The young man frowned and pulled his shirt down. "Maybe don't mention that if you ever have a chance to be my wingman."

"Right, a hundred and fifty stitches and you single-handedly exed the Axman," Vic joked.

Marco, however, was all for it. "He gets it."

Valerie sighed and shook her head. "I never want to hear that jackass' name again."

"No kidding," Annie agreed. "I'm not sure I even want

to see an ax at all. I think we'll change to those fireplaces you simply click on as advertised on TV."

"I certainly feel you on that." Johnny laughed and the others joined him before quiet settled. They were all in good spirits but it seemed, in this moment, that they realized it was all truly over. "So what are your plans now?"

Marco folded his arms. "Our folks are coming into town after all the hysteria."

"They don't know about how…involved we were," Annie added.

"They did see some footage when the fake Axman attacked and the fight in the parking lot, but they don't know about his obsession with Annie." He sighed and shook his head. "Honestly, I think we're gonna keep that from them."

"I can certainly understand. After everything ya'll been through, I would expect you'd want to put it behind you," the revenant conceded.

"Yeah, it's been a lot." Annie looked at Valerie. "What about you, Val?"

The officer shrugged and gestured to the precinct behind her. "I got one more day of downtime but after that, I'll be back in business and there's a shitload to get through. One of the nice things to come of this is an influx of cash into our department, courtesy of the SEA. Donovan thinks he can secure us some tech as well."

"Make sure they don't make you proxies," Vic cautioned.

She shook her head emphatically. "Not a chance. No one here would let them, but the plan is for the Agency to get the hell out of here once all the repairs are finished."

"Yeah. They probably know how much they fucked up," Marco grumbled. "If it wasn't for Donovan and his team, they probably would have done more harm than good."

"He seems like a nice enough guy," Johnny remarked and looked down the street at two Agency vehicles. "Although I wouldn't mind not seeing him or any Agency uniform for a while."

"And what about you guys?" Annie inquired. "Do you have more mysteries to solve and terrors to catch?"

Vic pulled his hat down. "Well, if there is a nice thing about this profession, it's the job security."

"We'll head back to Texas for now and maybe see if we can get something a little closer to home," Johnny added.

Marco tucked his hands into his pockets. "So where do you guys live?" He looked at Vic. "Figuratively speaking."

"A little place called Marfa," the revenant replied. "It's a weird little town but it's home and I got to work cases fairly early there."

"The rent's cheap too," Vic commented. "There are ghosts aplenty there—not always the nice kind but most aren't too malicious. Still, it keeps the real riff-raff out."

"I might swing by if I'm ever driving through," Valerie said. "I heard they have a nice festival going on there. Something about weird lights that appear?"

Johnny shrugged. "It brings in the tourist dollars. Most don't know it's only phantasma flare-ups from crossing points that appear in the area every year."

"Seriously?"

The ghost detective nodded. "Johnny keeps threatening to post an article about it and the tourist board pays an annual fee to stop him." He chuckled and nudged his partner. "He came up with that at fourteen. It was probably the first time I was truly proud of him."

They all laughed again, followed by the uncomfortable silence.

"It's weird, man." Marco sighed and ran his fingers through his hair. "I've only known you guys for a couple of weeks, but it feels like I'm leaving friends."

"Same here, buddy," Vic agreed. "I wish it had been under better circumstances but we probably wouldn't have as many interesting stories to tell, huh?"

"It's not like we can't keep in touch," Valerie suggested. "If I'm stuck on a particular case or something weird is going on, I know who I'll call for a second opinion."

"The first five calls will be free," Vic told her and earned another whack from Johnny.

"We're always available if you need us—assuming we aren't caught up in something ourselves," the young man amended

"And how often is that?" Annie asked.

The detectives looked at one another before Johnny turned to her. "It's fairly frequent, honestly. I promise to get back to ya'll as soon as we deal with whatever is trying to kill us that week."

She grinned. "We'll hold you to that."

In the distance, music began to fill the air. It was upbeat, swinging jazz mixed with marching band drums. They all looked to where a giant parade began to move down the street across from them. "A parade?" Vic asked.

Valerie nodded. "We have a few of them going on today. That is a jazz funeral."

"Who for?" he asked and studied a large float with

numerous flowers and beads and decorated caskets in the middle.

"Merely out of respect for the ones we lost," she explained and held her cup up in a toast. "We're accustomed to death in this city and prefer to grieve by celebrating the life of those we lose. Besides, with how many ghosts find their way back, we'll probably see at least a few of them again so don't want to look sad about it."

"Heh, it's not a bad way to look at it." The parade continued and the young detective glanced at the meter across the street. "Should we head out, Vic?"

The ghost nodded. "Probably. Otherwise, we'll get boxed in by the festivities."

The group followed them to their car. "Head up the north side. I don't think the parades pass through there for another half-hour," Marco recommended.

"You'll come back, right?" Annie asked.

"Oh yeah, even if it's only for the parties!" Johnny said as he slid into the driver's seat.

"But I'm sure we'll be back for business as well," Vic assured him and retrieved one of his new cigars. "There's always something going down in New Orleans, right?"

"Let's hope not for a while!" Valerie shouted over the hum of the engine as Johnny started it. "Thank you, guys, for everything!"

They all said their thank yous and goodbyes and the revenant pulled away, increased speed down the road, and took one last look in his rearview mirror to see them waving.

"Hey, Vic?"

"Yeah, kid?"

"Did you get many cases where you left a little sad that it was over?"

The ghost took a puff of his cigar. "Oh yeah, in different ways. But sometimes, that sadness comes from doing a good thing, meeting good people, and having to move on." He ashed the cigar outside the window. "That's not so bad, is it?"

Johnny smirked as he felt something come to his eye. "Yeah, it's all right."

They had managed to avoid the parades and were now out of the city. Neither minded that they had to cut through some backroads to get back on the right road. They had been silent for most of the ride, simply thinking things over and enjoying the peace for now.

"How long do you think the trip will be?" Vic asked.

Johnny considered it. "Definitely over twelve. Do you think we should make a stop in the middle?"

His partner opened the glove compartment, retrieved an ashtray, and ground his cigar out. "It doesn't bother me. You're driving. I don't want to have to possess you and whip the car around if you fall asleep at the wheel."

The revenant rolled his eyes. "When have I ever done that—except that one time in Tucson?"

Vic chuckled as he wrapped the remains of the cigar, placed them in the ashtray and, put it in the glove box. He looked up and tilted his head as he leaned forward. "Hey, slow down a second."

Johnny complied but didn't see anything that would

catch his interest except for a sign farther ahead. Then he noticed odd markings on it. He brought the car close and slowed to a stop. They both got out and examined it. "It could be decoration," he reasoned as they tried to make sense of the marks.

"With how shredded it is?" Vic snorted and pointed at it. "Besides, it's a speed limit sign. The government isn't a festive bunch."

"Call me hopeful." He decided the damage was claw marks of some kind. "Signs are metal, right? What the hell could do that out here?"

"Nothing you'd find in a zoo," his partner muttered. "I think they might be werewolf claws."

"Werewolf?" The young detective frowned at him. "Has a werewolf ever been seen in the States?"

"Not officially." The ghost pushed his hands into his pockets as he turned and examined the ground. "I heard about one in Chicago when I was a kid but I think it turned out to be some uppity retriever." He frowned and knelt quickly. "Kid, I found something."

Johnny looked at the massive paw print in the dirt. "From the way it's placed, it looks like it is headed back the way we came."

"To New Orleans," Vic agreed as he stood. He sighed and shook his head. "I won't say it again."

"They need a new unofficial motto," the revenant agreed and retrieved his phone. "I could always leave a text for Val to let her know something might be headed there."

The ghost nodded. "True. But if it is a werewolf, bringing one down could net us a nice payday."

Johnny twirled his phone in his hand. "I think Big

Daddy has a standing bounty on one for around twenty grand. We don't even have to bring it in alive."

"He did say he wanted more trophies, right?" Vic recalled. They shared a knowing look and scrambled into the car, turned, and headed back to New Orleans for a new investigation.

Honestly, they didn't even make it an hour out. There was always something going down in New Orleans.

AUTHOR NOTES - MICHAEL ANDERLE
NOVEMBER 18, 2021

Thank you for not only reading this story but these author notes as well.

So, I'm on a trip to Cabo San Lucas...via car.

Knowing I am going to have little time to write author notes, I thought I could use that as justification to get D'Artagnan to answer a question for me.

He hates to do anything but write.

I said, "How hard could it be? You are just answering a question about why you wanted to do this series. It isn't a trick author notes question, I promise."

And he did them. Sweet!

For (I think) the first time, D'Artagnan is answering a question in author notes.

QUESTION: What did you like about the Revenant Files idea and why did you want to write it?

ANSWER: Honestly, what got me writing this series was the desire to do something more supernatural without having to sacrifice the ability to do action and have fun characters.

I've attempted in my own time to try and do a straight-up horror story and it's a bag of mixed results.

I have a fascination with the story of the Axeman of New Orleans, one of the many 'Jack the Ripper' of X- or Y-type creeps from the early twentieth century. It was interesting and fun for me to blend a historical account with a supernatural and fantastical bent.

Further, I ended up enjoying Vic more than I thought. He was going to be more of a mentor figure who Johnny visited on occasion rather than their current status as two sides of the same coin.

The world of Limbo was fun to create. Obviously, most people just see it as a type of abyss or nothingness as that is generally how it is talked about or framed in other stories.

My thought was that perhaps a city or empire or something could be created there, but it would always be just a bit off and taking pieces and portions from different times in history.

I guess it is just another version of the "infinite void" that it is often seen as, is it really moving on if you got to a place that is built upon memories?

I think the entire idea of ghosts is fascinating. I'm on the skeptical side of things myself; the idea is both enchanting and terrifying.

I think that was another thing that set me off to make this series. If ghosts exist and they have the ability to come back to the land of the living or stay in their own afterlife, which would they choose to do? What purpose would there be in coming back if they couldn't interact with the world in the same casual way one does when they are living, how would the world react if there was definite proof of an afterlife of some kind?

Admittedly these questions are far heavier topics than I dive into in the story, but it set off a spark that got me started building a world.

I guess that's part of the reason we ask rhetorical questions. We aren't really looking for answers. Sometimes we do it just to see where we end up.

...

Thanks to D'Artagnan for dropping his thoughts for me to put into these author notes, and if you would like to see more in this series, please go back and review book one and let the world know!

Ad Aeternitatem,

Michael Anderle

BOOKS BY D'ARTAGNAN REY

The Astral Wanderer

(with Michael Anderle)

A New Light (Book One)

Bloodflowers Bloom (Book Two)

The Oblivion Trials (Book Three)

Revenant Files

(with Michael Anderle)

Back from Hell (Book One)

Axeman: Cycle of Death (Book Two)

Jazz Funeral (Book Three)

BOOKS BY MICHAEL ANDERLE

Sign up for the LMBPN email list to be notified of new releases
and special deals!

https://lmbpn.com/email/

For a complete list of books by Michael Anderle, please visit:

www.lmbpn.com/ma-books/